Time Bomb

VIBE *a Steamy Romance*

Series #4

Time Bomb

Lynn Chantale

4 Horsemen
Publications, Inc.

Time Bomb
VIBE a Steamy Romance Series #4
Copyright © 2022 Lynn Chantale. All rights reserved.

4 Horsemen
Publications, Inc.

4 Horsemen Publications, Inc.
1497 Main St. Suite 169
Dunedin, FL 34698
4horsemenpublications.com
info@4horsemenpublications.com

Cover by 4HP
Editor Muñeca Fossette

Library of Congress Control Number: 2022931340

Print ISBN: 978-1-64450-494-9
Audio ISBN: 978-1-64450-492-5
Ebook ISBN: 978-1-64450-493-2

Table of Contents

*C*ain McBride rushed through the marbled foyer and up the wide, winding staircase with its gleaming wood banisters to the last room in the carpeted hall. Never before had he been summoned to his father's home with such urgency. His father, Thomas McBride, was nearing 80 and was just as sharp as when Cain was a teenager. Much to Cain's wonder, Thomas knew all his son's schemes and secrets and never let him get away with anything.

And now, Cain had been summoned to his childhood home.

Multiple scenarios played through Cain's mind. Perhaps his father was dying from some incurable cancer. Or maybe a stroke would force Cain to put his father in a home.

Cain dismissed the latter. Thomas McBride had enough money to hire private nurses to care for all his needs.

Cain composed himself before he knocked on the door. He ran his hand down from his neatly trimmed hair to the crisp edge of his mustache until he reached the silk of his tie. He didn't want to look flustered.

"Come," came the hearty response to his knock.

Cain twisted the knob. His father didn't sound like he was in pain or ill health. Cain pushed open the wooden door. The scents of aged leather and expensive cigar smoke greeted him. The scents of his childhood and of his father. Cain stepped into the room and closed the door.

"Father" Cain glanced around the room. The mahogany gleamed. The desk and credenza glowed with a mirror shine. The furnishings hadn't changed, but the paint and carpet had. The walls were a soft blue, almost gray and what was once carpet now gave way to a deep charcoal laminate flooring. Cain had to approve of the look. It seemed more stately and masculine somehow.

"Here, son," came the deep voice.

Cain followed the low murmur to the small sitting room. The open balcony doors let in the late summer breeze. Soon, the weather would be too cool to have the doors open; instead, his father would keep the fireplace burning.

Cain stepped into the room with two easy chairs, separated by an antique table facing the fireplace. Above the mantle was an oil painting of the entire family: Cain's parents, five brothers and sisters, and a grandparent from each side.

He crossed the room and kissed his father on the cheek. His father's skin was papery and wrinkled, but there was strength and intelligence in those burning brown eyes.

"Good to see you, Cain!" He picked up a glass of iced tea. "Have a seat."

"You scared me. What was so important you needed me to rush over here?" Cain settled in the other chair, facing his father.

Thomas McBride sipped his tea as he gazed at the painting on the wall. "Do you know why I had that painting made?"

Cain looked at the picture as well. He opened his mouth to answer then closed it. Truthfully, he had no idea why there was an oil painting of their family. "No. I really don't."

"There's something prestigious about having a painting commissioned." A slight sneer was in the older man's voice. "I wanted to have an heirloom to pass down through the generations. Something to say Thomas Scott McBride was here, and this is his legacy." He nodded toward the print. "You and the rest are the reason we are as prosperous as we are."

Out of the six children, Cain was the only one to take a genuine interest in the family business: Baking mixes. From cornbread to pie crust, all the business's products could be purchased for less than fifty cents unless a consumer was purchasing a family-size box. McBride was synonymous with quality baking products and rivaled companies like Jiffy and Betty Crocker. Thomas was still Chairman and CEO, but Cain was his right-hand man.

"Is there something you want me to do with the company" Cain wracked his brain for anything from the last meeting that would've given his father pause. As far as he could remember, numbers were projected to exceed in the current quarter, and McBride's was on track for a record fourth quarter.

"All of you children have equal shares in the business."

Cain was bitter. His siblings had done none of the work. They had all interned and worked summers at the company. But Cain was the one who slaved in the mailroom, then humped it on the production floor. He scrubbed toilets and fixed broken machinery. He knew of every leak, crack, nut, bolt, berry, and cornbread at McBride's. While his older brothers and sisters were out with friends, Cain was learning everything he could about the family business. Even his time in the test kitchens had been well spent. Wasn't his Berry Berry Blast Cobbler one of the hottest selling things on the market? He'd done that. Who made sure marketing and PR performed the way they were supposed to? He did. He crunched numbers to make sure the workers were given a living wage while still turning a profit for shareholders, always bearing in mind his father's words: *Treat a man with respect, and he'll never leave you.*

And if an employee dedicated a good part of their waking hours to the company, they were compensated. McBride's was one of the few companies with employee longevity and very little turnover. Cain was so caught up in his accomplishments he nearly missed what his father said.

"I loved your mother fiercely," Thomas was saying.

"I know that?" Where was Thomas going with this?

"The only reason I'm bringing this up now is because I need to know what happened to her."

"Happened to who?"

Thomas sipped more tea. "Not long before I met your mother, I learned I had a daughter."

Cain gaped.

"That was my reaction as well." He offered a self-deprecating smile. "I've changed my will to include her into what she's entitled, but I need you to find her."

"Wait!" Cain exploded. "Wait just a minute! You call me here to tell me about some long-lost sister and that you've conveniently added her to the will. Oh, and you need me to find her."

"That's exactly it." Thomas replaced his glass. He turned to study his son. "Will that be a problem?"

Cain swiped a hand down his face. If only he could wipe away his feelings so easily. He let the silence linger, not sure how to put into words what his father had just told him. "Did mom know?" he finally asked.

Thomas nodded. "Your mother and I had no secrets from one another. She encouraged me to find the girl and introduce her to y'all."

"Father, you ask a lot."

"I need you to do this," Thomas said firmly. "This family has more than enough wealth to spread around. All of my children will get what they are entitled to."

Cain lowered his head so his father wouldn't see the blatant anger in his eyes. Sharing his inheritance with his siblings was one thing. Sharing it with a faceless woman who had no rights other than being born from a lucky sperm and egg was totally different. But he would do what his father asked, even if it was only to eliminate the woman.

"All right. I will find this woman for you."

Thomas patted his hand. "You're a good son, Cain. Knowing I'm leaving the company in your very capable hands pleases me to no end." A twinkle brightened his eyes. "You know a few of the grandchildren are interested in the business. Aidan has some interesting ideas for our social media accounts."

Cain puffed out his chest at the mention of his oldest son. Aidan was in his last year of college and used both his and Cain's experiences with the company to write his thesis. Being the first to find this mysterious woman would be a priority. His children, who were working or seeking to be in the family business, deserved a larger share.

"Great. And son?"

Cain met the old man's gaze. "Yes?"

"When you find her, bring her to me. I want to be the one to explain what happened."

Cain stood. "Of course. I'll get started right away."

As soon as he left the house, Cain pulled out his phone. "We have a situation."

"And that is?" his wife, Athena, prompted.

"My father wants me to find his long-lost daughter. And get this—he's already written her in his will."

⌒

Fa-ther Time. Fa-ther Time. The rhythmic chant swelled and bounced off the high ceiling. The voices continued to echo around the room. Father Time, an older black man with a shock of white hair and matching facial hair, ran from side to side in the squared ring.

He drank in the energy, absorbing the litany like an Orca after a Blue Whale. He loved this. Wind rushed past his face. Sweat trickled down the bridge of his nose, and he swiped it away with the back of his hand. The other hand held the championship belt he was placing on the line tonight.

Bounce. Snap. Thwack. Thwack. Bounce. Snap.

Father Time caught the briefest flash of blue, shifted on the balls of his feet, and darted for the three equally spaced ropes on his right. He stopped running the ring.

Chest heaving, he found the corner and climbed the first turnbuckle. Then the second. Balancing a foot on either side, he straightened, raising his arms in the air and waving the golden belt in victory.

If it were possible, the crowd roared louder. Chants of "Tick Tock" were interspersed with "Father Time." He beamed. He jumped down, ran to the next corner, and repeated his victory stance.

The match hadn't even started, and he had the crowd eating from the palm of his hand. This was the best thing he'd ever done. His entire life, he wanted to be a professional wrestler, and after surviving so many of life's tests and trials, he was living his dream.

He'd made it to the third turnbuckle when he heard a scrape of shoes. The crowd's chants and vibe changed as well. An edge of tension crept into the mix.

He hid a smile. One of the heels, a bad guy in the wrestling world, would be rushing in the ring any moment to yank Father Time from the ropes and body slam him to the mat.

A prickle of unease jangled Father Time's senses. A flash of warning. He jumped, but not fast enough. The metal caught him mid-thigh. The momentum knocked him off balance, and he fell toward the concrete floor.

Chapter One

Raucous laughter spilled from the open door of the bar. More patrons braved the lively crowd and warmth for an exciting evening. Abigail Anderson poured tequila into a shot glass before combining it with simple syrup. She placed the lid on the shaker, gave the drink a thorough shake, then poured the contents in a waiting glass. She carefully put a twist of lime on the salted rim. Next to the glass, she placed the pitcher of margaritas she'd prepared.

"Order up," she called. She quickly washed her hands and went about mixing the drinks on her ticket. Noise, a combination of laughter, music, and television, spoke of people celebrating life.

A grin creased her lips. *Just another Friday night at Abigail's.* A couple of nights a week, she played bartender. "Played bartender" wasn't an accurate assessment. She was a bartender. This was her place, and she loved mixing drinks. And the patrons, often surprised by the strength of her drinks, always tipped when she was bartending.

A receipt machine whirled and spat out a ticket. She ripped off the ticket and skimmed the paper with her fingertips. She still had the voice reader on as a backup, but she loved being able to use the braille printer when she could.

Each bottle of alcohol and mixer, as well as the pulls for the beers and soft drinks, were labeled in braille. Her staff had become proficient in the alphabet established by Louis Braille. Some staff members welcomed braille, especially on busy nights when they could rely on touch instead of sight.

She concentrated on mixing a martini and cosmopolitan. Tonight's crowd was a good thing. A few weeks before, she'd had to close the bar for repairs. Someone had decided to break not just the mirror behind the bar but several hundreds of dollars in booze and glassware. A few of the tables and chairs were busted as well. What concerned her most was that the police had no leads.

The intruder wore a mask and gloves. There wasn't anything distinguishable about him—other than that he was male. With that description, he could be anyone.

She'd since changed the alarm code, as it was the general one she'd given to a few choice vendors and a handful of Council for the Blind members. Now, those few choice vendors had their own codes, as did the few Council members.

Had she done that sooner, she'd have been able to tell who had vandalized her place. That was on her. She was just a little too trusting. She wiped down her area and returned the bottles to their proper places. The utensils went into a large rubber tote, and one of the dishwashers would come swap out the full tote for an empty one.

She moved to the end of the counter, reaching beneath the wood for her collapsible cane. The molded grip gave her pause. This wasn't hers. She patted the shelf again; this time, a smooth handle greeted her seeking fingers. She replaced the other. One of her guests from the last get-together must have left their cane behind.

With a flick of her wrist, the cane extended and locked into place. She maneuvered from the safety of the bar and headed toward the kitchen.

She and her late husband built Abigail's Place from a little hole in the wall, and they were never sure if they'd survive the first few years. With working 18-hour days, going to school, and raising three small children, Abigail was amazed their family had survived. But it had, as did Abigail's Place. The once shabby bar grew into its present configuration. Over the years, they'd added the restaurant portion. Nothing fancy, just a handful of bar foods and items to entice patrons to drink more. And the restaurant gave her an additional revenue stream when college students came in looking for a quick, filling bite to eat.

She always made sure there was a little something for the students. She could remember how hard it was being far from home and not having enough to eat. As long as students had a current and valid student ID, they received a substantial discount on their meal. Minus drinks, of course. Even *she* didn't give booze away.

"How we doing in here?" she called, walking through the swinging kitchen doors.

"Uh, we could use a little help on some prep," Brian called back. A sizzle nearly drowned out his words. "I haven't been able to get back and take care of it, and Kyle is running a little slow."

"I heard that," Kyle hollered.

Abigail hid a smile. She had some of the best employees. Brian was one of her managers, and Kyle was pulling double duty as line cook and dishwasher. She made her way closer to the action. Heat radiated on her left, as did the hiss and boil of frying foods. She kept walking, swinging her cane from right to left until much cooler air surrounded her.

"We're running low on some of the veggies," Kyle informed her. "Everything you need is stacked on the table to your right. I'm going to go catch up on the dishes real quick."

Abigail was well-acquainted with every aspect of the commercial kitchen. The prep area was a horseshoe, three sides lined with stainless steel tables. The walk-in was also to her right as was the magnetic strip which held the sharp chef's knives for cutting.

She washed her hands at one of many hand-washing sinks around the kitchen, donned an apron, and slipped on food-service gloves. Soon, she was wrist-deep in carrots, cauliflower, celery, and broccoli.

Her bar and eatery were her passion and dream. Her late husband, Jim, did everything in his power to make the place a success.

She blinked back the sudden tears. *Too bad you didn't live to see how great we've become.* After all this time, the pain of loss was still raw. Maybe not as sharp and jagged as it had been ten years before, but it still stung. No one could plan for an aneurysm. He'd gone with a friend to grab a case of wings. He went to sleep on the ride home and never woke up. She'd never have that type of love again.

"Wow!" Kyle said.

Abigail gave a tiny start at his voice. She'd been so caught up in her thoughts that she hadn't heard him approach.

"I'm sorry. I didn't mean to scare you."

She laid down her knife and peeled off her glove. "No worries. I believe I'm done."

Kyle chuckled. "I'll say. Thanks, boss. I can take it from here."

Nodding, she removed her apron and tossed it in the laundry bag. She took up her cane again. Now that all was well, she made her way to the office. This establishment put all three of her children through college. All three children may have grumbled about working after school and summers, but they all learned the value of hard work and how to save money. But only two of her children loved the restaurant.

She was proud of her kids. Clare, her daughter and youngest, was the only one to go on and do something different. She was an accountant. Her two boys, Brandon and JJ, James Junior after his father, both put in nights as waitstaff. Of course, they all had their own families, but in a pinch, any of them would come and help out at the bar. She looked forward to her children coming home for visits. They weren't a close-knit bunch, but they did love one another.

She unlocked the office door. A jangle of metal on metal made her smile. A moment later, a cold, wet nose bumped against her hand. "Well, hello to you too, boy." She gave the aging English lab a good scratch behind the ears. "Are you enjoying your break time, Percers?"

Percy, her guide dog, had been with her for the last nine years. Since he was nearing 11, it would be time to retire him soon. But she didn't see the need to do so just yet. Her pooch still enjoyed putting on the harness and going to work. She would work her dog as long as he wanted to work.

She plopped down in a chair and exhaled. She'd built the bar and raised her family, and now her heart ached as she realized she wanted someone to share it all with. She was quite content with her life, but she missed the day-to-day of having a male companion of the two-legged variety. And quite frankly, she was getting tired of replacing batteries.

With another sigh, she straightened and focused on the invoices on her desk. She fed them through a scanner which read the data aloud. From there, she could plug the numbers into the computer and compare the numbers against what had been emailed. As a final measure, her manager and daughter would make sure everything was correct.

A knock sounded on the door.

"Come in!"

"Uh, Abigail. It's Misty," said the feminine voice with a hint of an Indian accent.

"What can I do for you, Misty?"

"Uh, there's a man asking for you at the bar."

"Did he give you a name?"

"Something Time, I think."

A warm glow slid through Abigail. Swift was asking for her. "Well, show him back."

Misty closed the door without further commentary. Abigail fluffed out her long hair, then smoothed down the front of her polo shirt and jeans. Hopefully, there weren't any lingering broccoli or celery bits on the material. When she realized what she was doing, she laughed. She couldn't think of the last time she primped for a man.

A knock preceded the door opening. "Misty said it was all right for me to come on back," came the deep basso.

Abigail closed her eyes as the scent of musk and sage tempted her. "Sure. Come on in. Watch Percy."

Time came in and closed the door. "Is he in harness?"

"No."

Time's clothes rustled, and his voice sounded closer to the floor, indicating that he was kneeling. "Come here, boy," he beckoned. "Oh, that's a good boy."

Percy let loose one excited bark as his tags jingle-jangled. Abigail smiled as the dog's nails clicked and tip-tapped on the tiled floor.

"You have such a good dog," he praised.

"Have you ever thought of getting one?"

"I have, but I'm not ready for that type of responsibility."

Abigail nodded sagely. Indeed, having a guide dog was a huge responsibility. Maintaining the condition of the animal costs $900-$2000 a year, and that was just to cover food, monthly preventives, annual vaccines, and vet visits, along with any grooming needs. If the animal was sick or injured, the cost went up. Many handlers also didn't consider consistent training. Nothing huge. Just the basics to keep the dog sharp. Most guide dogs were preprogrammed with over 40 commands. As the handler and guide continued to learn, the list could become quite extensive.

Percy nudged her knee, and she stroked his sleek head. He rested his head on her thigh, almost as if he was offering her comfort. They'd been a team for a long time. She didn't know what she would do when it came time to retire him.

"You look so sad," Time observed. "What is it?"

"Oh, sorry. I forgot you could see."

He chuckled. "A bit. Or enough to see you're sad."

"It's nothing. Just thinking about my old boy here."

"He's just like us, still giving them youngsters a run for their money."

She laughed. "We sure are. So what brings you here, Swift?"

Metal scraped against the tile as the only other chair in the office was moved. "I thought I would ask you out on a date."

Flustered, Abigail did not speak. Heat crept up her neck and cheeks. *Was I that obvious in my attraction?* She enjoyed the company of the older man, who was a private investigator by day and a semi-pro wrestler by night. But wait a tick, how had she not known he was interested in her?

"I'm sorry." The chair scraped again. "I thought…"

"I'd love to go out with you," she blurted. "You surprised me is all."

⌒

Swift Time let his gaze linger on Abigail's slim oval face. Her long strawberry blonde hair was held back by a hairnet leaving her chiseled cheekbones unframed. Her sightless eyes were an intelligent brown fringed with long, thick lashes the same color as her hair. Right now, that marvelous face was tinged pink.

He reached over and covered her hand with his. Her skin was petal soft compared to his roughened palms. He could imagine the rest of her would be just as silky. This woman stirred something in him he hadn't felt in a long time.

Asking Abigail for a date had been a work in progress. Because of his occupation and affiliation with the Council for the Blind, he regularly saw Abigail but hadn't worked up the courage to ask her out.

He had beaten cancer, come back from strokes, and became the oldest wrestler. But he had trouble asking this beautiful vibrant woman on a date.

"So, where are you taking me on this date?" she asked, a mischievous smile playing over her full lips.

"I think I can manage dinner at Weber's," he returned.

She clapped her hands. "Do they still have the salmon pâté? That's one of my favorite appetizers."

"For you, I will make certain they have it." Pleasure stole through him when she squeezed his hand. He stood. She stood as well. "I should let you get back to work."

She moved her hand to his biceps. "You really do keep in shape."

"I do my best." Placing his hands on her waist seemed the most natural thing in the world. She was just tall enough for him to rest his chin on the top of her head. The scent of peaches rose around him as he inhaled her shampoo. She was soft, feminine, and trim. Not with the hard-toned body of someone who stayed in the gym, but with the soft curves of a woman not ashamed of her body. He stepped a little closer, testing her boundaries. Would she tell him to stop or let her go? Or would she let him press his advantage?

She swayed into him, her hands on his biceps. "Are you always this forward?" Her voice held a breathless quality that sent his libido into backflips.

"Give me a night where you're not busy," he said huskily. "We can get to know each other better over salmon pâté and a breadbasket."

"And if I want more than salmon pâté and a breadbasket?" She leaned into him.

He stepped away to claim one of her hands. He pressed a kiss to the knuckles. "You may have whatever you like." He felt behind him for the door. "Now, I'll let you return to work." He kissed her hand one more time and left the office.

As he walked, he unfurled his cane. He had a date with a beautiful woman.

The noise of the bar followed him as he wove his way through the tables to the exit. The air was much cooler and a little damp as he stepped onto the sidewalk. He paused to inhale a night full of fragrant food, exhaust, and the stale tinge of cigarette smoke. Ann Arbor was alive with pedestrians, bicyclists, and plenty of yappy dogs on leashes.

Music of all kinds spilled from open windows, doors, and clubs to create a myriad of clashing genres. Traveling down the sidewalk, he picked out blues, jazz, trash rock, and if he wasn't mistaken, polka music. He paused to listen. *Yep. Somebody is definitely listening to the Chicken Dance.* The scrape of the cane on the pavement added character to the night.

The blobs of shadow and color he could make out parted and swirled around him, giving him and his cane a wide berth.

Abigail actually said yes. For a moment, he didn't think she would agree to the date. He knew her history. He knew her late husband and frequented the bar once it reached its downtown location. And he had mourned when Jim died. Had he coveted Abigail even then?

The thought made him stumble. No. He hadn't even looked at Abigail like that. It was only in the last few years had he begun to see her as more than a friend. Truthfully, he hadn't had the best of luck with women. The two times he'd given marriage a shot, both ended in divorce. His first marriage lasted about five years, and his wife decided she couldn't handle being married and left him with their three-year-old daughter to raise.

Before the ink had dried on the marriage certificate with his second wife, he realized he was making a mistake. They'd parted ways with no hard feelings.

His phone vibrated in his pocket, and he stepped from the flow of pedestrians and stood near a wall.

"Father Time Detective Agency, where every second counts. Time speaking."

Silence, or rather the hollow whoosh of an open line, met his greeting. "Hello?"

"If I leave town, will you stop chasing me?"

Time stiffened at the quiet, unassuming voice. "Are you going to turn yourself in, Mr. VIP?"

Laughter floated and echoed. "That would be too easy for you. And I'm tired of making things easy for people."

Time pressed his back into the rough brick. He cast about for any threat and saw none. "What happened to you, man? How could you do that to her? She was just a baby."

"That baby tried to shake me down." VIP's sneer was evident in his voice. "She'd have hurt Geneva if I hadn't done something."

"You could've called the cops."

VIP made a sound somewhere between a snort and a laugh. "Right. Just like the cops did something about Winnie and my business? Everyone who died deserved what they got."

A flash, almost like a flash on a camera, skipped through Time's mind. He stood, trying to process the image of a mid-forties black man. His close-cropped hair was more gray than black. The glasses the man sported hung off his shapely nose. Both eyes were red ruins. "Dicky Williams," he gasped. Time drew in a breath. "You did that."

The Williams family had hired him months ago to find the culprit, but there hadn't been many leads. Now he could go back to the family and let them know he had found the responsible party.

"You knew him?" VIP asked in a cold voice.

"Of him. What did he do to you?"

"The philandering tech guy was no better than a man whore. He and my skeezy ex thought it funny if they ruined the blind guy."

If he'd been thinking straight, Time would've engaged his voice recorder. He patted his pockets. For once, the little recording device, no larger than an ink pen, was not in his pockets. Of all the days for him to forget an important device. Would he be able to coax another confession from Mr. VIP?

"I'm giving you notice, Time," VIP said.

"Of what?"

"I'm going to make my mark. So, Mr. Tick Tock, I'm coming for you. And I'm going to use any means necessary."

Time opened his mouth to respond, then closed it. VIP was no longer there. Time returned the phone to his pocket, leaned against the wall, and let the conversation filter through his mind. Even after all this time, he still couldn't believe his friend—a man he thought of as a friend—was a stone-cold murderer. Time pushed off the wall and resumed walking toward his downtown home office. He had a case he wanted to check—tracking down a woman's biological father. He didn't have much to go on, but something about the information nagged him like a splinter he couldn't remove.

Chapter Two

The night flew by. Abigail couldn't stop smiling. Now safely in her home, she unleashed and unharnessed Percy, who quickly ran off to slurp down water. She could hear the dog noisily drinking from her position in the hall.

She locked the door then placed the leash and harness on their designated hook. The only other sounds were the on-and-off hum of the refrigerator, the swish and bounce of the ceiling fans, and the A/C condenser. Quiet. Just like every other night.

She trudged to her bedroom. Slight tap-tap-tapping reminded her she needed to make a grooming appointment for Percy.

A soft whoop signaled the retriever had jumped on the bed, Percy's default location for as long as she could remember. Of course, he had beds and pillows sprinkled throughout the house, but he loved sleeping on the end of her bed.

She patted his head, and he licked her wrist as she paused. *He was such a good boy*. After a quick shower, she slipped beneath the cool sheets. Percy draped over her feet. His heavy weight offered more comfort than she realized she needed. If she didn't have the dog, she would be completely alone.

Again, she was reminded of how she wasn't afraid to be alone. She had the bar and its occupants to dispel any loneliness, but she longed for companionship. Would Swift give her that?

A slow smile creased her lips as she thought of Swift Time with his bulging biceps and easy laughter. She'd known him for a while, but only in recent years began to think of him as more than just a friend. She'd have to check her calendar for a date. If she had to take the night off to do it, so what? After all, she was the boss.

⌒

Swift Time stood in the foyer of the condo. Sergeant Falls stood in the middle of the empty space; the occasional crackle from the radio he wore on his belt provided his location. The only reason Time was here was because of the flash of vision he'd had last night. Swift continued to stand in the entryway.

The hairs on the back of his neck prickled as if someone was watching him. He didn't need to look around to feel the energy swirling and vibrating in the air. He closed his eyes to get a better sense of the energy. *Lingering emotions, maybe?*

"When we pulled her phone records, her GPS location had her here," Falls explained. "We're not sure if she was meeting someone about the unit or if she was trespassing."

Swift heard the voice as if in a tunnel. He was picking his way through the minefield of emotions. *Fear.* He inhaled. The sticky, almost palpable glaze of fear permeated the room. And with it ... a feral excitement.

He reached out a hand, his fingertips finding the swirls in the paint. He traced them over and over. The action was neither conscious nor deliberate. It was almost a compulsion he had to follow. *She did this. As she stood in this very hallway, she touched the wall and caressed the textured paint. But why did she come here?*

"Time? Are you with me?"

Time held up a hand. Excitement coursed through his veins, and the adrenaline rush of fear followed. *The certainty of death.* He moved through the space, unsure if he was tracing the perpetrator or the victim. Both emotions were strong.

Still, with his eyes closed, he traced the steps. He tilted his head. *Her.* He was following her emotions. He sidestepped, frantic to find an escape. There was none. His breath came in pants. He paused against the wall. If he could just...

Pain, not his own, exploded in his knees and abdomen. It felt as if he'd been slammed and held against the wall.

Again, his fingers went to the textured swirls in the paint. Tiny grooves met his fingertips. As blackness tapped at the edges of his vision, he seized and shook.

"Time!" Falls snapped harshly. "Snap out of it."

Time opened his eyes to stare into those of the sergeant's. For a moment, the brown eyes jumped and jittered into someone's else. Time closed his eyes, fighting to get away from the vision and orient himself to the now.

"Get me off this wall," he managed to say.

Falls led him toward the middle of the room. Time could breathe a little easier. The rush of emotions wasn't so bad now. "Okay." He nodded, then opened his eyes. "Okay," he said again. "She was killed here. Smothered." With a trembling hand, he pointed to the wall he'd just left to a spot about three feet from the floor. "She dug her finger-nails in there."

Falls crossed to where Time pointed and stooped to inspect the wall. "Well, I'll be damned," the sergeant muttered.

Time rubbed his temples. "If you don't mind, I'm going to step outside for a moment." Time hurried from the condo into the hall without waiting for a response. Much of the psychic energy followed, but it abated as he crossed the threshold. The farther he moved from the door, the less it became.

As Time moved toward the elevator, the energy spiked. He changed directions and headed for the stairs. He needed to breathe. He needed to get away from the ghosts and the pain.

For as long as he could remember, he knew and could see things before they happened. And often, like now, he could feel and see what had happened. He was never sure what triggered his extra gifts, but he'd learned to work with them. He had refined his talents by becoming a private investigator and a consultant for the police when they had no other leads.

He didn't bill himself as a psychic detective, but he'd earned the reputation for being one. All he did was use what he felt and saw to help others. When he wasn't doing detective work, he kept up his wrestler training.

After what he'd seen and felt, he needed a good hard workout to feel alive again.

Footsteps crunched on the gravel behind him. "Did you check with the realtor?" Time asked.

"How did you know it was me?" Falls asked.

"You smell like coffee." Time shrugged. "Did you check with the realtor?"

"Serefina Gellar did not have an appointment with the realtor. The owner could've set a private viewing."

Time held his breath. He needed to ask the next question, but he didn't want to hear the answer. "Who was the owner?"

"Vector Integrated Practices. The names on the paperwork were Rodney and Winifred Kimball."

Mr. VIP," he sighed.

"Yeah!" Sergeant Falls sounded surprised. "Do you know them or him?"

"I'm acquainted."

"From the preliminary background, he's lost everything. Wife, businesses, and his home."

Time scrubbed a hand over his face and beard. He wanted to be wrong. He really wanted to be wrong about Rodney being Mr. VIP. "Are you sure?"

"Like I said, it's preliminary. I'd have to do more digging myself."

Just like Time was going to do. "If you don't need me anymore, how about dropping me at my office?"

"Sure thing." He moved to Time's side and offered him an elbow. "So, when's the next match?"

Grateful for the change in subject, Time smiled. "Looking for tickets for the family?"

"Thanks for the offer, but it's not necessary. The kids love to watch you work the ring."

The keyless entry beeped twice, clicked, and the doors unlocked. Time opened the passenger side and slid in. A moment later, Falls joined him.

"I think in two weeks. There's going to be a Tag Team match with Perfect Storm, Casanova, a few others, and yours truly will be there."

Falls steered the car, bumping over a few speed humps before finally leaving the parking lot and maneuvering into traffic.

"You keep me posted. I'll even try to get some of the officers to bring their families. I know several of them are into wrestling."

Time grinned. "We're always grateful for new fans."

Swift Time sat in his desk chair, staring at the two 27-inch monitors. A stilted male voice read the text on the screen as he followed along. Everything he ever wanted to know about Rodney Kimball was right there in the public record.

Mr. VIP Vector Integrated Practices, a solid tech company that built solutions and software for the blind, took a significant hit over the last few years. The company, which had been on track to make over a million dollars, barely scratched a quarter million.

Time frowned and jotted a note to dig into the company's financials. He went back to the public records. Here was VIP's dissolution of marriage, company, and home.

Time kept scrolling and found the attorney of record, Gareth Bedford, Esquire of Hastings, Bedford, and Associates. He briefly wondered if Amelia had known about Rodney's life falling apart. Swift whistled. Rodney lost everything, and on top of that, he had to pay child and spousal support. He scanned the pages looking for the reason for the divorce. And there it was:

Infidelity.

Swift leaned back and rubbed his beard. A tingle ran up his spine as he recalled the phone conversation he had with Rodney.

Opening another window, Swift accessed his files on one Richard "Dicky" Williams. He scrolled through his notes, noting how a few of Dicky's colleagues mentioned a woman he'd been seeing.

Yes. There was the description. It could've been Winifred Kimball. He moved to how Dicky had died. Someone threw acid in his eyes before slitting his throat. If that weren't enough, Dicky's eyes were poked out, leaving behind a body so mutilated only a closed casket was in order.

Is that a nod for coveting someone's wife? Or something else? Time opened a second page on his web browser. He typed in Dicky's name, and two more small business owners popped up. One for a companion care company. *Interesting. It seems the woman who owned the companion company was also Dicky's wife.* Then there was Sherry—S is for Food catering. *Could Rodney have done all of those as well?*

A slap of cold struck him. *Murphy Giles? Had Murphy been Rodney's victim?*

With shaking fingers, he picked up his phone and dialed Sergeant Falls.

"Miss me already?" Falls teased.

Wind rushed through the line. "Got a question for you."

"I might have an answer."

"Giles? Was he a homicide?"

"Uhh. I can check, but I thought it was ruled a heart attack."

"If there was an autopsy, I need a copy of the report."

"What is it, Time?"

"I think Rodney may have killed Giles."

A knock sounded on the wooden door. The frosted glass vibrated in its frame.

Time sighed. He didn't have any appointments. "I'll have to call you back." He hung up without saying goodbye. "Come in," he called.

The knob jiggled as the hinges squeaked open. Time would need to fix that unless he decided to get some chimes. The office wasn't that big, just large enough to stash a desk, a file cabinet, and two chairs, one of which he was sitting on. He also had a tinted window large enough for him to jump out of. He knew because he'd tried.

A man, wrapped in a tattered windbreaker of some indecipherable color, was wearing slacks so shiny that Time wondered why he couldn't see his reflection in the fabric.

"Mr. Time?" The man sounded wispy and hoarse as if he had sustained vocal cord damage.

"Yes."

"I'd like to hire you."

"For?" Time prompted. A faint tingle skittered over his awareness. This man wanted something, but not what he was asking.

"I was hoping you could find some items for me."

The tingle worked up to a sizzle. "What kind of items?"

The man approached the desk and gestured toward the chair. "Can I sit?"

"I don't know. Can you?" Time quipped.

The man gave him a blank look.

Time sighed. "Have a seat."

"I had a safety deposit box in a bank that was robbed a few months ago. I want those items back."

Time pursed his lips. He hadn't heard of any bank robberies, but he didn't pay much attention to anything that didn't happen within the city limits. Mentally, he rolled through his caseload. He didn't think he had time to commit to another case between training for his wrestling matches and the handful of cases he had. Not when he was determined to find Rodney. And woo Abigail.

"As much as I would like to help, I'm a little busy." He opened drawers, searching for the right card. He held the card close, peering through the lens of his glasses with one eye closed. Yep. It was the right one. He scribbled his name on the back.

"Try them. They're in a strip mall downtown. Across the quad. They have more staff and resources."

The man took the card, staring at it. "True Detective Agency?"

He smiled. "Tell them Time sent you. They'll give you a discount."

As the man rose to leave, another knock sounded on the wood. The man smiled. "Are you always this busy?"

"They always say time flies when you're having fun," he quipped.

The man's eyebrows drew together in confusion, then brightened. "Oh. A joke." Now he laughed something between a teakettle whistle and a burp.

Time shook his head. *The man wasn't too swift on the uptake, and he had a peculiar laugh.* "Good luck to you."

The man doffed an imaginary ha, as an average-height woman with overly tight curls and too much bronzer slipped past. She waited until the door closed before she sat in the lone visitor chair. She placed her leather handbag on her lap; her posture was rigid and ungiving.

"Mr. Time," she began, enunciating each letter and syllable in a cool, flat tone. "I engaged your services more than a week ago, and I have not seen any results."

Time pasted what he hoped was a pleasant smile on his face. The nicety did little to relieve the mild aggravation simmering. "Mrs. Johnstone, I informed you when I took your case that gathering information would be slow. You're asking me to find a person from the mid-twentieth century. If the person is still alive, he would be well into his 80s."

Her ruby red lips thinned. "But I need to know. All my life, I've been told my mother was my mother, and my aunt was my aunt. And to learn that my aunt is, was," she corrected, "my mother is very disturbing."

He leaned forward, pushing the box of tissue closer to the woman.

She pulled out a few and dabbed her eyes. "Thank you."

"Have you spoken to your mother, I mean aunt, about this?"

"The woman who raised me suffers from dementia. Whenever I ask, she mumbles and changes the subject," she said with some bitterness.

Time steepled his fingers as he arranged his thoughts. "Do you know if either woman kept diaries or journals? Old letters? Anything to help point me in a direction other than the family name?"

Mrs. Johnstone opened her bag and removed a stack of papers tied with ribbon. These she sat on the desk. Time leaned forward and retrieved them, realizing they were envelopes, yellowed by time. A few were stained with what he hoped was water. He turned over the packet, seeing strong but faded lettering addressed to a Miss Edna Woodward. He brought the missive close attempting to decipher the return address in the upper lefthand corner. Failing, he removed a magnifying glass from the center drawer and tried again. He could just make out the name Thomas Scott. He laid down the glass and letters.

"Have you read any of these?"

Mrs. Johnstone shook her head. He was mildly impressed when not a single strand of curl moved on her head.

"No." She stood. "I hope you can get me some answers. I'd like to know who my real father is."

Time stood too. "Of course." He skirted the desk. "Allow me to walk you out."

When Time returned, he sat and carefully untied the ribbon. He counted the envelopes—seventeen in all. With great care, he pulled out the first letter. The paper was thin, nearly transparent, but still legible.

He made it through three of the letters before a jolt of electricity zipped up his fingers and flashed in his brain. The image was grainy, like an old black and white film. A couple. A tall man with chiseled features and haunted eyes stood straight despite the brace around one leg. The rounded-belly woman held the look of a younger Abelene Johnstone. The other woman, this one also resembled Abelene, except she was a little heavier and disapproval deepened the lines of her face, tugged at the pregnant woman's arm. The man lifted a large, dark hand and placed it on the baby bump. Shifting, he allowed the other hand to cup the younger woman's cheek.

Overwhelmingly hot and raw emotions threatened to suffocate him. Time breathed deciphering grief, heartbreak, love, fear, and—he licked his dry lips ... jealousy? Not from the pregnant woman, but the other. Edna and Ginny. The names popped in his head. The man, Robert. No, Rufus. No, Thomas.

The invasive shrill of a telephone sliced through the vision. Time dropped the letter and sat back, gasping for air. He sucked in several breaths before his hands stopped shaking. The emotions and residual adrenaline lingered.

The phone rang again. Time snatched it up.

"Father Time Detective Agency."

Silence. Heavy breathing.

"Hello?"

A soft click, then the buzz of an open line.

Just what was that about?

Time moved to return the letters to their envelopes when the phone rang again.

Chapter Three

A bigail chewed her lower lip as she listened to the ringing on the other end. Someone picked up after the third ring. "Time."

The rich baritone tickled her ear and warmed her right down to her toes. "It's Abigail."

"Abigail."

She heard the smile and something else through the phone. "Is this a bad time?"

A slight hesitation. "No. Just sitting at my desk."

"So, you're working?"

"Not really. Putting my desk to rights before I leave for practice tonight."

"You sure?" she blurted. "You sound a bit off."

"Sometimes, I see visions. They leave me a little drained."

"I've always been curious about what you see."

"Really?" Wariness and interest filled his voice.

"It has to be such an amazing gift and a terrible burden to know things before they happen and be unable to prevent them."

"Yes, that's it exactly. But I do what I can when I'm able."

"You are so amazing," Abigail praised. "I can see you tomorrow night."

"Wonderful. I'll make a reservation for 7 pm and have a driver take us there."

"Are you sure you don't want to drive?" she teased.

He laughed, a deep rumbling sound that went straight to her toes. "One day, when they perfect self-driving cars, you and I will cruise the strip."

"I'd like that."

"So would I."

"Hey, mom!" her daughter Clare called. "Where are you?"

"Swift, I have to go. My daughter is here."

"I look forward to tomorrow night."

"Me too." Abigail hung up the phone before either could say anything else. She couldn't wait until she had a chance to visit with Swift. Before going to bed tonight, she'd have to check the restaurant's website for its dinner menu. She couldn't remember if they had one online or not.

"Mom?" Clare called again. "I thought you were ready."

"I am." Abigail picked up her purse. "You are early."

"I finished early and didn't want to start anything new." A note of censure hung in the younger woman's voice.

Abigail paused. "If this is inconvenient for you, I can do this another time."

As much as Abigail loved her children and enjoyed spending time with them, they often acted inhospitably or like she was a burden, like now.

A huff coincided with a foot stomp. "I told you I would be here, and I'm here. If you keep stalling, you'll have to ride with me to pick up Oscar."

Abigail brightened at the mention of her grandson. "I don't mind that. How is my little sausage man?"

"Don't call him that."

"He likes it."

"He's too young to know what it means."

"But he's such a cute little round guy. Reminds me of a little sausage."

At four, Oscar was a little roly-poly and cute enough to eat.

"Are you bringing the dog?"

"Percy," Abigail called. "Percy."

A moment later, dog tags jangled, and a wet nose brushed Abigail's outstretched hand. "Wanna go to the store, boy?" She held up the leash, and he walked away. "Guess not." She returned the leash to its hook and picked up her cane.

"He's really looking like an old man," Clare said. "His eyebrows and chin whiskers are gray."

"Really?" she asked in some surprise.

"Yep. I've got the door."

Abigail made sure the door was locked then made her way to the passenger side of the SUV. She was fastening her seatbelt when her phone rang.

"Yes," she answered, thinking it was one of her managers.

"Did I catch you at a bad time?" Amusement clung to the rich baritone.

"Oh, Swift. Not at all." She couldn't stop the rush of heat into her cheeks. "What can I do for you?"

"Do you have a favorite color?"

Of all the things he could've asked, that wasn't what she expected. "Pink."

She could feel Clare's eyes watching her. Her blush deepened.

"All right. See you tomorrow evening."

Abigail disconnected the call.

"Well, I don't think I've ever seen you blush like that before? Is that a suitor for my mother?" Clare demanded.

"It's just dinner."

"Do I know this man?" Clare backed down the drive.

"Swift Time."

Again, Abigail felt the weight of her daughter's stare.

"Um, weren't you guys friends a long time ago?"

"Yes," she said, relieved that she didn't have to describe who Time was.

"Were you cheating on daddy with him?"

"What? No!" Abigail exclaimed. "What a horrid thing to say."

"And he's Black."

"What does his color have to do with anything?" Abigail demanded. "I raised you to respect and treat everyone how you'd like to be treated." Whatever good feelings she'd experienced from Time's call were gone. She couldn't believe how narrow-minded and rude her daughter was being.

"That's not what I meant. I have several Black friends."

"Do you know how ignorant you sound right now? Maybe you need to stop listening to the more extremist news stations."

"Mom, really. You need to know about these things. Especially at your age."

Abigail turned her face to the window. "Let's just get this over with. You won't have to worry about me asking you for a ride to the store." She knew her daughter had more conservative views, but to hear such remarks come out of her mouth was just...

"We're here," Clare stated a few minutes later.

Abigail punched the release for her seatbelt. Her hand was on the door handle when Clare touched her arm.

"Mom, I'm sorry." Clare shifted in the seat. "You surprised me."

"There are better ways to express your surprise," she admonished. She pushed herself out of the car, extending her cane. "If anyone else heard you say that, you'd come off racist."

"I—" The door slammed. "You're right. Hey, wait up."

Abigail was halfway across the parking lot and to the automatic doors when Clare caught up to her.

"Goodness. I forgot how fast you could move." Clare gave a breathless laugh as they walked through the doors together.

Cold air swirled around them. Overhead, an instrumental version of Lionel Richie's "Hello" played. The scent of apples and cinnamon diminished the farther they walked from the doors.

"Do we need a basket?" Clare asked.

"No. I only need a couple of skeins to finish the blanket I'm working on."

"Do you know the color?"

Abigail smiled. "They're holding them at the counter for me."

Clare steered them in the direction of the counter. The faint chime of the card reader met her ears.

"You're next in line. While you're doing this, I'm going to see if they have some paint I've been looking for."

Before Abigail could respond, the slight breeze lifting her hair let her know Clare had left. Abigail stood until she was called. She moved her cane back and forth until it hit the counter.

"I thought that was you," a tenor, male voice announced.

Abigail furrowed her brow, trying to place the voice. "Austin."

"At your service. Are you here with your assistant today?"

"My daughter."

"Did you have to bribe her?" Austin asked, his voice dropping to a conspiratorial whisper.

Abigail chuckled. "Next time, I'll bring my assistant."

"So, what can I do for ya?"

"I called ahead for some yarn," she explained. "Judy said she'd have it at the counter for me."

Plastic crinkled, and papers rustled. "Yes, she did mention you were coming in. Well, not you specifically. But she was holding yarn for someone." His voice moved, growing louder and softer before finally settling right in front of her. "Had she told me it was for you, I'd have had it ready. Here, feel."

Abigail accepted the chenille-like softness. She loved the velvetiness of the baby yarn. "I love working with this. It's stretchy and warm. And when you wash it, it keeps its softness."

"Absolutely. Is this for the blanket you're donating to the raffle?" The scanner beeped.

"Yes."

His clothing rustled as he leaned forward and lowered his voice. "Next time you come in, bring about ten tickets. I'd like to further the cause."

"Thanks." She shifted her purse, digging through the bag for her wallet. She counted the cards, felt for the tiny dot on her debit card, then handed it to Austin. "We got a new system," he began. "Let me come around the counter and show you. Since you have a chip on your card, it goes here."

He guided her hand to the slot for the card. "And we'll run this as credit."

Clothing rustled again, and keys tapped. The reader chimed a trill ding-ding-ding.

"And you can pull out your card."

Abigail removed the plastic and placed the card back in her wallet. "That wasn't so bad." She held out her hand for the bag.

Austin laughed. "I had a hard time learning the system."

"Understandable."

He laughed again. "Have a good one, Abigail."

Abigail swiveled. Bag in one hand, cane moving back and forth in the other, she walked toward the sound of whoosh and sliding. She stood to one side of the automatic doors to wait for her daughter.

Her mind wandered to the last few months and all that had happened. The most recent of events, the car explosion, occurred a mere block from her bar. The accident had overshadowed Murphy Giles's wake. She rubbed her shoulder against her cheek. As much as she'd found the man annoying, the meetings were not the same without him.

The automatic doors whooshed open. Humid air pushed in. Someone gasped a deep breath, and she was shoved hard.

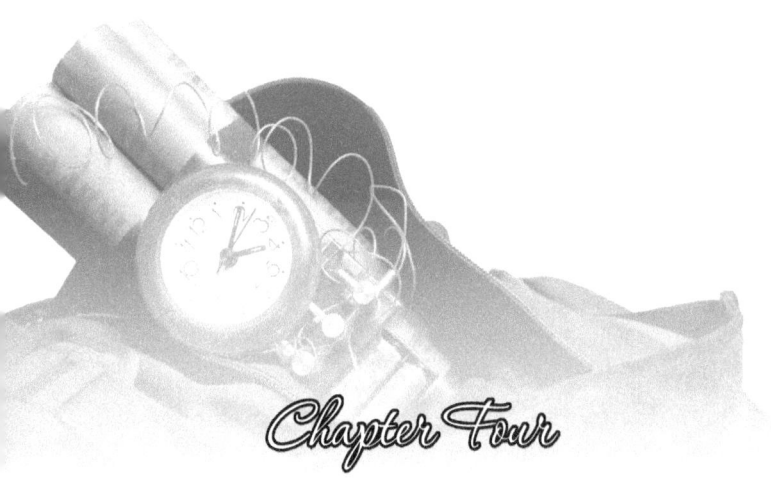

Chapter Four

"Time!" a familiar voice exclaimed.

"Moses." Time accepted Moses Hawke's proffered hand. The former football star and wrestler had a firm, almost crushing grip. Moses's long, honey-colored hair was swept back from his chiseled, angular face. Time settled his gym bag on a nearby chair. "How's the wife and kid?"

The chiseled, angular face split into a wide grin. "She is doing just fine, and so is the baby."

Time sat and rummaged in his duffle for his knee and elbow pads. "She's due any day." He made it a statement instead of a question.

"Any day," Moses echoed. "Get warmed up. I'll tell you what I have in mind for the next match."

Time went through a series of stretches. Sufficiently warmed, he rolled beneath the last rope of the squared ring. Time's joints gave a cursory pop as he rose to his feet. He bounced on the balls of his feet, the padding and boards bending and flexing to accommodate his moves. Now he ran the ring, bouncing into the ropes and using momentum to propel him to the other side. Turnbuckles creaked, ropes stretched, and boards and padding cushioned each footfall.

Time swiped at the sweat dripping into his eyes. Without his glasses, his vision was blurred and shadowed. He paused in one corner, rotating his shoulders. Vibrations shook the ring and traveled through the rope as Moses faulted into the ring.

Time followed the shadow, bouncing as Moses landed. The two men circled one another. Moses made the first move. The two came together in a collar-elbow lockup where Moses gripped the back of Time's neck with one hand and his elbow with the other. From there, Moses transitioned to an armlock. Time countered, using the other man's momentum, and sent him into the ropes. Moses returned. Time caught him by the arm, shifted his weight, and tossed Moses to the middle of the mat.

The loud thud echoed off the rafters. "More hip," Moses informed him. Panting, he stood. "You need a little more snap when you do that hip toss." They went through the toss again. "Great. Now let's work on your Time Bomb."

The Time Bomb move was a modified suplex, requiring the men to be either chest to chest or chest to back. Time tossed Moses's arm over his shoulder, gripped the waistband of the man's pants, and lifted him straight up. If this were a match instead of practice, Time would let the man fall to the mat. As it was practice, Time allowed Moses to stand.

"When you do this move, get as high as you can."

"Right."

They went through the "Time Bomb," then worked on the correct way to clothesline an opponent. While the move could be dangerous and cause significant harm to an opponent, done correctly, no one would be hurt. Moses demonstrated, placing his forearm against the broadest part of the chest, just below the collarbone. To the spectators, it would look like he caught him in the throat. They also worked on headlocks. "All right, old man. Show me what you got."

Cain stared at the non-descript barn, hearing faint thuds and grunts from the inside. He'd observed an older black man strutting into the building an hour earlier. Now, Cain debated whether to continue his vigil or make an appointment. He wanted ... No, he needed to know how much information this man had on his family.

Cain shrank into the shadows as the tires of a dark, late model SUV with a limousine sticker on the back window crunched the gravel. The same vehicle had dropped Time off earlier.

He walked back to his own SUV to wait. He'd follow and find where Father Time lived.

Abigail let out a gasp as she fell into something hard and metallic. Her left, then right side exploded with pain as small heavy objects rained down on her.

"Mom!" Clare screamed from somewhere above her.

Gasps and pounding feet vibrated through the floor. Unsure of what had happened, Abigail didn't dare move. All she knew was that everything hurt.

"Hold still," Austin said. "I know it's uncomfortable but let me remove the figurines from you."

Austin tossed small, heavy bits, presumably from the figurines, to the side as he spoke. Abigail laid in an uncomfortable position. Stiff metal bit into her ribs, hip, and thigh. She would be black and blue for her date tomorrow night.

She choked back a giggle at the absurdity of the thought. She should be more concerned about who pushed her rather than how she would look for her date.

"Are you okay?" Austin wrapped a strong arm around her waist, extracting her from the debris on the floor.

"Oh, Goodness, Mom." Clare ran frantic but gentle hands up and down Abigail's body. "Oh god. She's bleeding. She's bleeding."

"If you can walk, my manager will take you into the office," Austin began. "We have a first aid kit there."

"What happened?" Clare demanded.

People moved about her, touching and asking questions. Clare tugged Abigail one way while someone else chatted about what they'd witnessed. Abigail needed a minute to process it all.

She stepped forward and realized she didn't have her bag or cane. "My bag and cane."

"Don't worry about that now," Clare admonished.

Minor aches and pains introduced themselves to her body. The loudest ones were a burning pain near her elbow and forehead. She felt a warmth trickle down the left side of her eye. She was bleeding. *Maybe I can arrange my hair to cover the bruise for my date.*

She nearly laughed aloud. Here she was, doing it again, worrying more about her date with Swift than the issue at hand. "Just look at you," a female voice piped up. "Come. Let's get you tended to and find out what happened."

Several agonizing moments later, Abigail, Clare, and Patsy, the manager, sat in the quiet office. Someone pushed a bottle of water into Abigail's hands as she sat.

Drawers opened and closed. Papers shuffled back and forth. "What happened?"

"Someone shoved me," Abigail answered.

"What?"

"I was waiting for my daughter when the doors opened. The next thing I know, I'm hitting hard stuff, and more heavy things are falling on me."

"Hold still, Mom. I want to clean this cut."

Cold whispered along her hairline before it swelled into a burning sting. She winced. "What is that? Acid?"

Clare chuckled. "Alcohol."

Keyboard keys clicked and clacked. A moment later, Patsy gasped. "I think it would be best if we reported this to the police."

"It wasn't an accident?" Abigail asked, the first hints of apprehension settling in her stomach.

"No." The chair squeaked as it rolled away. "Sit tight. I'm going to grab the names and numbers of the witnesses."

Mr. VIP stalked his way down the sidewalk. *Stupid. Stupid. Stupid.* Time had him so off his game, Mr. VIP was making stupid mistakes. But what else was he supposed to do when he saw Abigail standing near a shelf full of tiny pumpkins, ghosts, and other Halloween knick-knacks? He had to give into his impulse to shove her. But people had seen him.

He marched quickly up the concrete and into another store in the strip mall. He skirted the front end where the registers were located and made it through aisles of towels, sheets, lamps, and other home goods.

He paused. No longer visible from the front and near enough to the back of the store, he could listen from the employee-only area.

Voices drifted and rolled from the front. VIP edged closer to the stockroom area and heard footsteps squeaked toward, then away from him. He listened, holding his breath. No other sounds emanated from the back of the store. As unobtrusively as he could, VIP slipped into the forbidden area.

Shapes and shadows met his wandering gaze. He needed to get out of there before someone caught him. He carefully picked his way through the stocked boxes and shelves until he came to a metal door with a push bar. He hoped an alarm wouldn't sound if he went out. Even if it did…

He stopped as flickering lights drew his attention. *Monitors. Where there are monitors, there are cameras.*

Damn! He really was off his game.

Pulling out his phone, VIP hurried to the desk with the computer and hard drive. He paused. A voice floated to him. Frantically, his gaze darted around the setup. *Is this cloud-based or something old-school like discs and VHS tapes?* He found his answer—a memory card.

With a smile, he ejected the little card, no bigger than his thumbnail, and pocketed it. With a last look around, he hurried out the emergency exit door.

No sound emitted other than a chime. If anyone tried to look at who'd been in the store, they'd get nothing.

He exited into the back parking lot designated for over-flow parking and deliveries. He found a nearby sewer grate and dropped the memory card into the abyss. A tiny splash met his ears, and he walked away whistling. Too bad he hadn't planned better at the craft store. If he had, no one would have seen his face.

Chapter Five

Abigail sank up to her chin into the warm, lavender-scented Epsom salt-laden water. Every bruise and aching muscle wept in gratitude. She leaned her head on the padded cushion and sighed.

She still couldn't believe someone shoved her in a very public place. What especially boggled her was the description of the man. Average height, thick glasses, fortyish, and angry. She shook her head. *It couldn't be him.* The last time she'd seen him was at Murphy's wake, and he'd been just as surprised as the rest of them at Murphy's death. What reason did Rodney have to hurt her?

She lifted a hand from the water to brush a damp curl from her cheek. Of course, rumors were floating around the Council about what *really* happened to Rodney's business and marriage. Abigail gleaned, from the bits and pieces she'd garnered over the last few months, that Rodney's wife, Winifred, left him for another man. That man was then murdered.

Abigail shifted in the tub, water sloshing around her. That would've been about the time Winifred stopped coming to the meetings with Rodney.

She sank a little lower in the tub, soaking in hot water in a vain attempt to minimize the soreness from her tumble. She hoped she would look at least eighty percent better before her date the following night.

And there it was again. Abigail was more concerned about how she would look for Time than why Rodney thought it prudent to assault her.

Maybe it was an accident? Or perhaps he thought he bumped into a display rather than a person? She chewed her lower lip. *No. That doesn't make sense. He would've stopped and apologized, not run away.* Based on witness accounts, Rodney had walked in, shoved her, and ran out again.

With a sigh, she sat up. Cool air raced across her heated skin, and she shivered a little. Nails tip-tapped across the bathroom tile. A moment later, a cold, wet nose nudged her shoulder.

"Yeah, yeah," she muttered. "I'm getting out." Abigail pressed the switch with her toes to let out the water and stood. She reached down to her left to retrieve the large fluffy towel from the closed toilet lid. She stepped onto the bathmat as she toweled off and gingerly blotted her injuries. Once dry, she debated smearing a topical pain reliever on the worst of the aches but decided on a couple of aspirin instead. She pulled a super soft cotton night shirt over her head and stuffed her arms through the sleeves.

A jingle of tags and soft thump on the foot of the bed signaled Percy was in his favorite spot. Abigail smiled. She did love that pooch. Would Rodney have attacked her if Percy had been with her?

She snuggled beneath the sheets and light blanket. Between the bath and the pain killers, she felt comfortable and tired. She stifled a yawn. *Tomorrow will be soon enough to figure out the rest of the world.* Even better, she had a date with Swift Time.

___

Music and laughter drifted on the breeze as easily as the scent of cumin, turmeric, and grilled meat. A few pedestrians littered the sidewalk. A couple of teens raced down the cement on skateboards, the noisy wheels clattering as the teens performed tricks. Traffic moved back and forth on the cross street ahead. Swift Time paused in the fading shadow between the buildings and scanned the street. Nothing seemed out of place. Yet there was something...

He felt the prickly sensation of someone watching and slowly surveyed the area. Across the street, a car pulled out of the paid parking lot as another car circled for an open spot. A group of bicyclists walked their bikes through the crosswalk. He pivoted to look back the way he'd come. He took note of the three restaurants on his side of the street. The nearest and farthest restaurant had outdoor seating. The one in the middle had a bright yellow awning with "Le Shish" in a loopy script.

Movement caught his peripheral, and he tracked it to a young boy in black skinny jeans and an oversize black tee. He followed the boy's progress until the boy disappeared in front of the post office on the opposite corner. Time continued forward, jogging up the six wide, shallow steps of his intended destination.

He knew he was still being watched. Time pushed open the heavy glass door to the Ann Arbor Public Library. Cool humidity enveloped him, as did the scent of leather, paper, and somebody's pizza. He paused long enough to make sure he wasn't being followed. *No one.*

He watched the street for a few more moments. The prickly sensation faded. Whoever was watching was gone now. He turned back to the next set of doors and pushed through. The open foyer was well lit. As he crossed the lobby, he was aware of a group of teens circling the waist-high drawers to his right. From previous visits, he knew music discs waited inside. Ahead and to his right were shelves housing mystery fiction and new titles. He bypassed the shelves to his left that held requested materials for patrons as well as the wall shelf stacked with complete seasons of new and old televised shows and movies.

He continued past two elevators and staircases. One staircase led to the upper floors; the other led to the basement and meeting rooms. He stood at the threshold of the reference room.

To his left were several computer stations. The quiet clicking told him that a few computers were occupied. He continued forward until his cane tapped the front of a wooden desk.

"Mr. Time," a slightly nasal tone greeted. "What brings you to my neck of the woods?"

"Gretchen, I hope you can lend a hand on some research," he began. "I'm hoping to put together a rough family tree."

Chair wheels scraped across plastic as clothing rustled. "For yourself or a client?"

"This is for work."

Gretchen rounded the desk then headed to the far side of the room. Time followed, and they passed rows and rows of nonfiction books, maps, almanacs, and even a huge globe in a gleaming wooden frame.

She stopped in front of a microfiche machine. A computer sat beside it.

"The library has access to some of the ancestry websites. So, we'll start there." She placed a hand on the back of the wooden chair. "Would you like me to begin the search or give you time?"

"Let me see what I can find first. If I need anything, I'll let you know."

She nodded. "Very good. I'll be back in a bit to check on you."

Time sat in front of the computer, set out a small pad of paper and a 20/20 pen. The pen was similar to a marker but made thicker, bolder lines. The pad contained white paper with bold, black lines that made writing easier for Time to see and read.

Carefully, he set about looking for Thomas Scott.

Swift Time dropped his notebook on his desk, and the few papers he had tucked and folded in the back fell out on the surface. He gathered quite a bit of information on Thomas Scott and his family. He would have to see where the living relatives were so he could speak with them. That would be his task for tomorrow. Now he noticed the 8x10 envelope in the basket of his mail slot. He got up and retrieved it, a little surprised at the heft. He undid the little string and upended the contents. A few photos fell out. These he set aside facedown. He didn't need to see the waxen, lifeless face of the man who'd been his friend. Time was only interested in what the medical examiner found.

Time read the autopsy report. The ME hadn't found anything suspicious other than a bit of latex between Murphy's teeth. The ME figured either the first responders or the bus driver who found Murphy unconscious left the latex.

But what if it wasn't either?

He'd warned Murphy to be careful. *What if Murphy was the first successful blind person VIP killed?* Time sat straighter in his chair. *It would make sense. Penelope was hurt in a fire at her bakery.*

To this day, the man accused of setting the blaze denied his involvement. *What if the man was telling the truth?* Then there was Amelia. Someone had placed a poisonous snake in her bedroom. Rodney had been on the property previously, along with a few other people who wanted to see Amelia hurt. And then there was Geneva. Someone had mugged her but hadn't tried to kill her. *Or had they?*

He stood, stretching his weary muscles. The wrestling practice from earlier was making itself known. His joints creaked and popped as he flexed to loosen the stiffness. He opened and closed his fingers. A touch of arthritis left them sore and achy, and he'd forgotten to take his pain meds that morning.

Crossing to a short filing cabinet, he pulled out the top drawer. Inside was a small metal box with a fingerprint reader. He placed his thumb on the scanner, and the lock clicked. He lifted the lid and retrieved a copy of Serefina Geller's file. He took it back to his desk and pulled out a magnifying glass. He squinted through the lens at the photo of a smiling young woman. Her wavy brown hair framed her lovely face. At first glance, she looked a lot like Geneva Martin. He set his phone next to the photo and pulled up a picture of Geneva. He looked from one to the other, noting the similarities and differences.

Geneva's hair was lighter and had some highlights Serefina's hair did not. Their faces had the same general shape. Serefina's chin was more pointed, while Geneva's was more rounded. Geneva also had a more delicate look about her. And the most obvious difference was that Serefina had eyes, while Geneva did not.

Time set the glass aside. *What if Rodney took out Serefina instead of Geneva?* After his little outing at the condo, he was certain Rodney murdered Serefina. *But why?*

Leaning back in his chair, Time laced his fingers behind his head. A tingle of awareness flowed through him, and he reached a hand for the telephone. A second before it rang, he picked it up. "Father Time Detective Agency, where we make every second count."

"The phone didn't even ring," a warm, feminine voice greeted.

A smile creased his lips when he heard his granddaughter's voice. "Cammie. How are you?"

"I should be asking you that question," she said with a chuckle. "I keep getting images of you in the ring getting hit with a steel chair."

Time laughed. "Sorry about that. I've got a couple of matches where the chair is involved."

"You sure?" Doubt crept into her tone.

Time paused. While he got occasional flashes of the future or images of the past, his granddaughter could almost summon visions on command. She often only had to touch an object or have someone touch her to know something about them. The closer her relationship was with the person, the more detailed her visions were. "I'm sure, sweetheart. Will I see you at the next match?"

"Absolutely. The café is closing early that night just so we can support you."

"Really?"

"Yes. A lot of my regulars bought tickets and are bringing their families. So, you should have a packed house." She turned serious. "Seriously, Pawpaw. Be careful. There's a really nasty dude gunning for you."

Some gifts just keep on giving. "I'm always careful, sweetheart."

"I know, but this guy is bad. He's hurting, so he's hurting everyone around him."

A chill squiggled down his spine. *Is she talking about Rodney?*

"And he sees you as an obstacle to his goal."

That was the same impression Time had. "I will be careful, but you can't wrap me in bubble wrap."

She snorted a laugh. "The only thing that will do is make you squishy. Make sure you hone those wrestling and self-defense skills."

He chuckled. "I had training with Moses tonight and again tomorrow."

"Love you, Pawpaw."

"Love you too." With that, he hung up, a grin still on his face. His granddaughter was worried about him. Concern wasn't something she regularly displayed, so for her to call and warn him meant she'd seem something drastic. Her warning, along with his visions, confirmed that he was on the right track. He would stay vigilant.

He would contact Sergeant Falls in the morning to see if he had any additional information regarding the autopsy and place a little bee in his bonnet regarding the other three unsolved murders. Time hesitated and picked up his phone.

"Set a reminder."

"What would you like me to remind you of?"

"Contact Penelope, Amelia, and Geneva regarding their mishaps."

Reminder set, he plugged in the device. He wondered if Abigail was still awake. He glanced at the large, bright numerals on the digital clock. It was well past midnight. It was too late to call, but he would call Abigail in the morning. He had an overwhelming urge to know how her day went.

The next morning, Time could hardly wait. He could no longer ignore or deny his urge to speak to Abigail. As soon as he heard her greeting, he knew something terrible had happened. "What is it? You don't sound right."

"Then you probably should see me. I'm black and blue all over."

"Where are you?"

"Home at the moment."

"Stay there."

Twenty minutes later, he rang the bell at Abigail's sweet little ranch-style home. He stood inside a screened-in porch that offered a nice view of the neighborhood. A bench, a little oversized for the space, sat to his right, and a large, fabric-lined wicker basket sat beneath a mail slot.

Three sharp barks brought his attention back to the door.

"Quiet, Percy!" Abigail admonished. The dog continued to bark. "Quiet, or I'll get my squirt gun." The barking ceased as the locks nicked back.

What Time saw broke his heart. And his reaction was only based on what he could see. The left side of Abigail's face, just below her hairline, was bruised and swollen. Dark stripes and lines marred the softness of the skin on her arms. "Oh baby," he breathed. "What happened?"

"Come on in." She held out a hand for his.

He grasped her fingers. They trembled a little in his. Time allowed her to pull him across the threshold.

"I've made coffee. Go ahead and help yourself." She locked the door.

He turned her to face him. A tingle of electricity surged up his arm, and he gasped.

The unexpected shove. Falling. Pain exploded all over his body. *Not his body. Hers. The bastard shoved her.* He stepped away, letting his hands drop to his side.

"He's going to pay for this," Time vowed.

"I'm okay, Swift." She shuffled into the kitchen.

The house was an open concept home. The living room, dining room, and kitchen formed one sweeping view. The morning sun filtered through the sliding patio doors off the dining room. The spacious kitchen was to the left. The island curved, creating a barrier between the living and dining room. Stools sat beneath the eat-in counter reserved for informal meals.

"Did you see what happened to me?" she queried with a note of awe in her voice.

"Yes. It doesn't happen all the time, but I saw what happened."

"Can you predict the lotto?"

He smiled. "I think my granddaughter can. Her gift is much stronger than mine."

Abigail reached for a mug, wincing. Time hurried to her side. "Here. Let me get that." He removed two mugs from the cabinet. "Sit at the table," he told her. "Is anything broken?"

She shook her head. "No." With a sigh, she sank into a chair. "But I'm too old to go shelf surfing."

He snorted at the dry humor. "You take your coffee black, right?" He poured the dark brew into the mugs. He added a splash of cream to his.

"You remembered."

"I pay attention." He brought both mugs to the table. Hers he set near her right hand.

"Be careful. It's very hot." He went back to retrieve the plate of muffins he'd seen. Seeing that the napkins were already on the table, Time sat across from Abigail.

Abigail wrapped both hands around the mug. Her hands shook as she raised the coffee to her lips. "I can't believe Rodney would do something to hurt me." Sadness eked through. "I asked my daughter, and she was sure it was him."

"Where were you?"

"At the craft store picking up more yarn. I was standing near the door when it happened."

She reached a hand out to cover his.

A flutter of awareness zipped through him. Abigail was reaching out to him for comfort. He glanced at their hands. His were dark cocoa, rough and a little ashy; her hands were slim and soft. He could lose himself in the very texture of her hands.

"Why would Rodney want to hurt me?"

Time sipped his coffee as he arranged his thoughts. How much of the truth should he tell her?

"You know something," she prompted.

"I do," he agreed. "I believe he hurt you because he's hurting. Rodney has lost everything he's built."

She gasped. "Oh no. So the rumors are true?" She reached for a muffin. "I've heard some gossip at the social events. None of them I believed, but I did hear about the divorce."

"It's more than just the divorce. His wife took their daughter, stating he would be an unfit parent because of his vision."

"That's horrible and so not true. Rodney adores Candace. Heck, he was there when Winifred was out doing God only knows what." She broke off a bite of muffin and popped it in her mouth. "But Candace has to be about 17 now. Surely she has a say in where she lives."

"I can't give you all the details. But since Rodney lost his home and business, the judge sided with Winifred."

"Oh, that woman makes me want to find her and slap her silly."

"I bet you would, too," Time said with a chuckle.

"Of course, I would. Rodney's a good guy. At least he was until he pushed me into stuff."

Time chewed a muffin.

"I've been meaning to ask you. Did you leave a cane at the restaurant? There's one behind the counter that isn't mine."

Thrown by the sudden shift in conversation, Time didn't answer. Instead, another jolt of electricity surged through him, and his ears rang. Shattering glass filled his vision while the scent of alcohol rose around him.

Her gentle hands squeezed him, and a pretty face swam before his eyes. He blinked several times, bringing Abigail's concerned face into focus. "I'm all right."

"You went so quiet there. I thought something was wrong."

Time breathed deeply, holding her hand as tightly as she held his. Her touch anchored him to the now. Awareness and a spark of desire flitted through his bloodstream and pooled low. His body's response surprised and intrigued him. He'd had his share of women, but this type of visceral response to Abigail pleased him.

"Are you still feeling up to dinner tonight?" He hoped she would say yes but would be flexible if she said no.

"Absolutely." She withdrew her hand. "Would you like more coffee?"

The warmth and energy flowing through him seemed to leave with the absence of her touch. *Is the rest of her as soft and sensuous as her hand? Will her touch be gentle or firm? Does she taste as good as she smells?*

His desire to sample her lips pulsed and throbbed. Time shifted his erection to a more comfortable position. He didn't think he'd been this hard in several years.

"I think I'll pass on the coffee," he said hoarsely. He cleared his throat. "Did you bake these muffins?"

"Yes. When I get time, I usually whip up a batch. Then I freeze them until I'm ready to bake them. It's wonderful for when company drops by."

Her chair scraped, and the table shimmied as she bumped it. "Sorry."

"Nothing spilled." He selected another muffin. "Do you serve these in the restaurant?"

"Sometimes, but it's something we usually reserve for restaurant week." A couple of times a year, Abigail participated in Taste of Ann Arbor, a week-long event that highlighted several restaurants and bars in the area. A restaurant-goer could receive a meal, from appetizer to dessert, for a flat fee. She and her staff always showcased the best the bar had to offer. She even included a signature drink and a coupon.

"You'll have to let me know when you make these again."

Abigail stood and picked up her empty coffee mug. Swift rushing over to make certain she was okay made her body course with pleasure. She carried her mug to the coffee maker and poured half a cup.

No one had done that in a long time. And Time had been concerned enough to call off their date if she'd been too sore or tired.

What startled her was the way he'd gone still and quiet. For a moment, it was like he wasn't even in the room.

"Have you always been able to see visions?" she wondered.

"Yes."

"Does it bother you?"

"No one has ever asked me that before."

She returned to the table and sat in the chair next to his. For some reason, she needed to be close to him. She allowed her hand to brush and linger against his arm before moving away. *He always smells so good. Crisp, clean, and masculine.* She settled fully in the chair, shifting until her knee deliberately brushed his. He wore jeans, the material soft from multiple wears. He surprised her by rubbing his knee against hers.

A ripple of desire swept through her veins. She hadn't been this close to a man she found attractive in a long time. Would he object if she laid her hand on his thigh?

"Thank you for coming over to see about me."

"I hope you don't think I'm too forward, but I already think of you as my lady."

Heat crept into her cheeks. "And we haven't even had our first date."

He placed a hand on her thigh. The heat from his palm radiated up and down her leg straight to her core. "Do we really need to date?" His voice was husky. "We've known each other a long time."

She stroked his arm, relishing the firmness of his biceps. Her late husband had been fit, maybe a little pudgy around the middle, but his arms were never as hard or as big as Time's. "At least one or two," she teased. "I wouldn't want you to think I was easy."

Time laughed, a deep, hearty sound that wound over and through her, much like a mug of rich, hot chocolate. Abigail could imagine listening to his laugh for the rest of their lives. She swayed a little at the thought. Just his laugh made her think of a "happily ever after." It was a scary thought when she knew a "happily ever after" could end in a breath.

Callous but gentle fingers caressed her cheek. She turned into the work-roughened palm.

A simple touch made her melt and wish for more.

"We've seen a lot." His breath was warm against her cheek. "I need to kiss you." He suited words to action.

The world faded to the pressure of his full lips on hers. The kiss was tentative, seeking, questioning. A leaned forward in answer, giving, responding, taking. His unique flavor blended with the taste of coffee and sweetness from the blueberries. Time tangled his fingers in her hair, holding her for his exploration. She allowed this, relishing the heat exploding through her veins and rushing to every erogenous zone. Her nipples tightened, her belly flipped, and desire dampened her panties. She moved closer, pressing her body into his. She draped an arm around his shoulders, her fingers bunching in surprisingly soft hair. Curls and waves scrolled beneath her fingertips as he deepened the kiss. He dragged her into his lap. From somewhere, dishes rattled on a hard surface while wood edged against her back. His erection pulsed below and between her legs.

She rocked against him, drawing a ragged gasp from him. Or was it her? *And we are only kissing. Kissing!* She hadn't been this turned on since the early days of her marriage.

"You're killing me!" Time stated when he released her mouth.

She dropped her head on his shoulder, panting and breathing him in. She swept her lips to the pulse at his throat. She flicked her tongue over him, and his erection jumped beneath her. She chuckled.

"That's not helping."

"Has this been between us all along?" she mused. She gently untangled from him and reoccupied her chair.

"I think it's been simmering, just waiting for the right time to bubble over."

Drip-drip-drip.

"Oh, dear." Abigail skimmed a hand over the table and found the source of the noise.

One of the mugs was on its side. She hastily grabbed a handful of napkins and sopped up the liquid. She carried the wet towels to the trash then retrieved the dishcloth from over the faucet. Returning to the table, she wiped up the rest of the spill.

"Did we break anything?" Time asked.

"Not at all."

His footsteps whispered over the tiled floor. A moment later, a low buzz filled the air. He must have grabbed the WetJet to clean the floor.

"Would you like more to drink?" She carried the dishes into the kitchen. When she turned, he was right there. "Oh."

"I want you, Abigail." He backed her to the counter, caging her between his muscular arms and body.

She tilted her head back, feeling the warmth of his breath on her face. "I want you, too."

"Good. We'll have dinner tonight and see what kind of dessert surfaces." He slanted his mouth over hers. The kiss was just as hungry as before, but a promise rode beneath the lust.

He stepped away, leaving her bereft of his heat and touch.

"Until tonight."

The door opened and closed a moment later, signaling Time's departure. Abigail touched her kiss-swollen lips. *The man sure knows how to kiss.* With an easy smile on her face, she walked into her room to ready the outfit she'd wear to dinner. It would be something easy to take off.

Chapter Six

Time sat in a rather uncomfortable chair in a roomy but stifling office. Video monitors sporting the logo of Dicky's A/V Company covered an entire wall. The logo almost looked like a "W" inside a circle with an antenna and remote attached. Time watched the letters come together in one big emblem before it blew apart and reformed in each of the twelve screens—four down and three across. It was nicely done.

"Sorry to keep you waiting." A young man with a deep voice and shoulder-length dreadlocks walked into the room. He pushed a pair of black round-rimmed glasses up onto his nose. He had a wiry build with well-defined muscles.

"Mr. Time," the young man smiled. "I take it you have something for me?"

Time offered what he hoped was a sympathetic smile. "Were you able to reach the rest of your family?"

Shaking his head, the young man sat. "My mom is coming, but my siblings are not interested in what happened to him." He flicked a piece of lint from the knee of his khakis. "The family fell apart, or should I say, my siblings didn't think our father was right in how he left our mother."

"Understandable, DJ." Time placed a file on the table. "I'm hoping my findings will bring you a measure of peace."

"So, you found who killed my father?"

Tip-tapping along with the shuffle of feet reached Time's ears. A moment later, an attractive woman appeared. A bright floral scarf held her long sisterlocks at the nape of her neck. Her companion, a beautiful yellow lab, kept tip-tapping.

"Hey, Mom." DJ stood then guided her into the only other empty chair in the room. "Mr. Time, this is my mother, August River."

"Nice to meet you, Ms. River."

"Likewise," August replied.

"Who's your friend?" Time asked as the dog lay at her feet.

"This is Riley," she answered, stroking the dog. "I'm getting him ready for his new handler."

"I've never seen you at the Council meetings," Time said. "We hold events several times a month. As a matter of fact, we've got one coming up this weekend."

"I do need to get out and make new friends," she said quietly.

"Time's a wrestler," DJ spoke up.

"Really?"

"Yes. If you come to the event this weekend, I'll tell you all about it."

A smile faltered on her lovely features. "I hope you're not flirting with me."

Time coughed. "No. As attractive as you are, I have a very nice lady I'm taking to dinner this evening. She's blind and owns a bar."

"Oh."

"What's the news you have for us?" DJ prompted.

"I can tell you who murdered your father and his ... uh ... wife."

"But the police haven't been able to find any more leads," August said.

"I'm not the police," Time retorted. "Your son hired me to find who took his father away, and that's what I did. His name is Rodney Kimball, and I believe he's killed a total of five people and attempted three more."

"But why?" asked DJ. "Why my dad?"

"He, your father, as near as I can find, was having an affair with a woman. This woman used funds from her husband's company to help bolster your father's. When the woman's husband found out, he killed him."

"And that's an honest-to-God life lesson on why one shouldn't cheat," August said with such bitterness that Time felt a tingle of electricity flow through his body.

"Mom, it's okay."

She patted his hand. "You're such a good son. I'll leave you to finish up with Mr. Time. I need to take Riley out for a walk. I will also let your siblings know what happened." She stood. and the dog came to life with a shake. "Mr. Time, please give the information about the meetings to DJ. I would like to attend." She left the room.

"They were married for over twenty years," DJ explained. "The whole high school sweetheart deal. She's still grieving the loss of that relationship."

"Understandable."

"She's also raising their young son, Isaac. Well, my dad's wife's son. My dad isn't the father, but he chooses—" DJ paused to regain his composure. "He chose to be the legal dad. My mom couldn't have any more kids, so she's been a second mom to the little guy since before he was born."

"Your mom sounds like a strong and compassionate woman."

"She is." DJ went behind the desk. He studied the file a moment before he removed a checkbook. Once done writing, he tore off a check and handed it across. "Thank you for finding the answers we need. I needed," he corrected. "Will you give your findings to the police?"

Time pocketed the check. "Yes."

"Good. I want to see the man behind bars. No one deserved to die the way my father did."

Time stood. "I agree." He removed a card from his pocket and scribbled on the back. "This is the time and place of the event this weekend. I hope to see August there."

DJ grinned. "I'll bring her myself."

Without a backward glance, Time left the office. As he exited the building, a flash of light blinded him.

Pfft-pfft-pfft.

He pivoted, dropping into a crouch. Glass shattered overhead.

Pfft. Pfft. Pfft.

More glass shattered, and someone screamed.

Time rolled behind a large concrete planter. Footsteps pounded, and the vibrations pulsed through his body. Tires squealed as a car door slammed.

"Time! Mr. Time!"

Time slowly lifted his head just enough to peer over the barrier. Tiny shards of glass shimmered like deadly diamonds. Sirens wailed in the distance. Time made it to his knees by the time DJ reached him.

"I called the police." DJ offered his hand.

Time allowed the younger man to pull him to his feet. "What happened?"

"I think someone was shooting at you."

Chapter Seven

Abigail smoothed the skirt of her dress down. The soft silk shimmered and swirled around her knees. She adjusted the bodice, trailing her fingers along the low neckline to ensure the lacey, strapless bra was not visible. Satisfied with her appearance, she dusted a bit of blush on her cheeks and applied matte lipstick. Years of practice honed her cosmetic application. She even managed to apply a bit of eyeshadow to her lids. She set the make-up brush aside for a perfume bottle. She squirted perfume, a subtle fragrance with hints of rose, orange, and spice, on her throat and wrists. The scent made her feel sexy.

She needed to know she looked fine for Time. Reaching for her phone, she debated on calling her daughter. Even though Clare would be honest, Abigail didn't want to deal with her daughter's negativity. Abigail had enough nerves. Maybe one of her sons? Or their wives? She dismissed that idea because she wasn't ready to answer questions. That left one person: her assistant, Caitlin. Abigail engaged the FaceTime feature on her iPhone and waited for the ring.

"Abigail," the warm female voice greeted. "Wow! You look great."

Abigail beamed. *So far, so good.* "Thanks."

"What can I do for you?"

"You did it. You said I look great." She willed the heat in her cheeks not to show. "I have a date tonight and wanted to be sure."

"Oh. How nice. Anybody I know?"

"Swift."

"You sly thing. He's a sexy piece of man candy."

Abigail chuckled and made a noncommittal noise.

"Hold the phone out so I can get the whole picture."

Abigail did as instructed, turning in all directions so Caitlin could see as much as the screen would allow.

"Your makeup is perfect. Your dress is beautiful, and your hair shines," Caitlin gushed. "Don't break his heart."

"I won't," she laughed. "Thanks." With a promise to give Caitlin an update, Abigail ended the call. She'd just dropped the phone in her evening bag when the doorbell rang.

Percy managed a soft woof.

"Are you sure you don't want to go to dinner with me?"

A soft thud and the click-clack of nails hurrying to the front door was her answer. Abigail smiled. Looked like they were both going on a date.

Quiet music from a live piano, muted conversations, and the tantalizing scent of rich foods and warm bread perfumed the air. Abigail skimmed her hands over the Downysoft tablecloth, then fingered the petals of the bouquet on the bench next to her. The flowers were a pleasant surprise. Their sweet fragrance enveloped her.

"Thank you again for the flowers," she murmured. "It's been a long time since anyone has given me any."

Time covered her hand with his. "I will make sure you have some on a regular basis."

She ducked her head as heat crept into her cheeks. She was acting like a lovestruck teenager rather than the mature woman she was.

"You look absolutely amazing tonight," he continued. "You always look amazing, but you're radiant."

His thumb caressed the back of her hand, igniting the butterflies in her belly. "That means a lot coming from you. And you're well-dressed this evening."

"What gave it away?" Amusement lit his voice.

"The hard heels of dress shoes. I also felt the soft wool of your jacket and the silk of your tie. The starch on your shirt wasn't unpleasant either."

He laughed a warm hearty sound. "You never cease to amaze."

"The amazing part would be to tell you what color you're wearing."

"So what color am I wearing?" he teased.

"Navy blue jacket and a red tie," she responded.

"Close. The tie is blue stripes." Material rustled. "At least I think it's blue. It could also be black."

Now she laughed. "Can't see those colors either?"

"Finally, someone who understands," he said in mock relief.

Footsteps approached. "Have we decided what to order?" The male voice was tinged with a hint of Spanish.

"Ah, Pablo. Good to see you."

"Very good, Time. And may I say your date is absolutely gorgeous."

"She is," Time agreed. He shifted toward Abigail. "Are you ready to order?"

"I think so."

They placed their orders, and Pablo promised to return with bread and plenty of salmon pâté.

"So, what happened after you left my place?" Abigail smeared some creamy appetizer on a slice of bread. She bit into it, and the savory fish danced across her tongue. She couldn't stop the moan of delight from escaping.

"You really do enjoy the salmon," Time mused, laughter in his voice.

Heat crept into Abigail's cheeks. "Yes. I've tried hard to duplicate their recipe, but it's always a little bit off."

"Nothing wrong with a woman enjoying her meal." He dropped his voice so only she would hear. "I hope you can enjoy me the same way."

She nearly choked on her bread as the memory of Time's taste replaced the morsel in her mouth. *Would the rest of him taste the same?* Suddenly, she was ravenous, and it wasn't for the coconut shrimp she ordered.

At that moment, Pablo returned with their meals. He set steaming plates in front of each of them. They waited for the server to leave.

"I managed to wrap up one of my cases today," he said as his fork and knife scraped his plate.

"Oh?" Abigail scooped up some of the wild rice with a spoon.

"Yes. You're familiar with Dicky's A/V?"

"Of course. They did, and do, a lot of work for the bar."

"I met my client's mother. She trains dogs, and I invited her to the social this weekend."

"That's wonderful. We can always use more people."
Abigail ate the rice.

"While I was there, I think someone shot at me."

Abigail's spoon clattered to the table, followed by a minute of silence. Time cringed. He wasn't doing this right. He was causing Abigail to worry, and he could feel the concern pouring off her.

She moved to rise.

"What are you doing?" he demanded.

"I need to see that you're okay?"

He grabbed her hand before she could move around the table. "I am. Sit down."

Lips trembling, she sat. If he wasn't mistaken, tears glimmered in her brown eyes. He could kick himself for putting those there.

"I had a premonition as I was walking out the door," he explained. "I was in more danger from flying glass than anything else."

"Don't sound so flippant!" she admonished. "This is serious. You could've been hurt. Or worse, killed. And then I would mourn you," she said with a hitch in her voice.

He took both her hands in his. "I'm sorry," he said gently. "It's been a long time since I cared for someone the way I do. Or have someone care about me the way you do."

"I do more than just care about you, you old fool."

He grinned. There was his feisty woman. "You're right. I was being an old fool. Now I know someone is after me."

She leaned forward, pitching her voice low. "Was it Rodney?"

Time placed her palm along his cheek so that she could feel his frown. "I don't believe so. This person was in a car.

And once the police arrived to take a report, they didn't find any bullets."

"So, what did they shoot at you with?"

"Ball bearings."

Her hand fell away as she sat back. "Ball bearings?" She skimmed the table for the dropped utensil. Time nudged it toward her seeking fingers. "Are you sure it wasn't Rodney?"

"I thought that until I heard a car speed off." They resumed eating. "Rodney doesn't drive, and I doubt he would have an accomplice."

"If you don't think it was him, then who?"

Time cut a bit of his steak. *That is a very good question.* Mentally, he ran through the open cases on his docket. There wasn't a lot. There were a few background checks, a couple of missing persons, and the Williams murder. Because of his personal stake with Rodney, or Mr. VIP, the Williams murder was the only dangerous thing going on. "The only case I had of any substance was the Williams case, and that has been resolved."

"But he's still out there."

"And the police know who he is."

She sat straight, a shrimp halfway to her mouth. "Really?"

"Yes. I gave them the information I had. They have to find Rodney now."

"So, if it wasn't Rodney, who was shooting at you?"

The evening was pleasant with a cool breeze and a kiss of humidity. Time and Abigail stood on the sidewalk, and Percy waited on Abigail's left side. Sparse traffic from the nearby highway and streets filtered toward them. When

Abigail shivered, Time removed his jacket and settled it on her shoulders. She pulled the garment closer, bending her head to place her nose to the lapel. He turned back to the parking lot with a smile on his face. "I know what you're doing?" she accused good-naturedly.

"Oh?"

"You're trying to make me fall in love with you. It won't work."

He bit back the sharp sting of disappointment. He almost missed her sly smile, but then hope surged anew. He snaked an arm around her waist. "And why not?"

"Because I'm already in love with you."

He dropped a kiss on her upturned mouth. "And I with you."

Twin beams of light bounced toward them. Time stepped in front of Abigail, and she chuckled as he shielded her with his larger body.

"What?"

"You're protecting me."

The car slid to a halt at the curb in front of them. The door opened, and a 40ish man in a leather cabby hat, white dress shirt, and black tie stepped from the vehicle.

"Mr. Time," he greeted, skirting the vehicle to open the backdoor.

"Jeff."

"How was dinner?"

Time stepped away as Abigail and Percy entered the vehicle.

"Wonderful." He slipped into the seat next to Abigail.

"Good. All in?"

At the affirmative, Jeff closed the door. A moment later, he was in the driver's seat.

"Where to?" Jeff asked, looking in the rearview mirror.

Time smoothed a lock of hair from Abigail's cheek. "Nightcap at my place?" he queried.

She smiled. "Mine.

"You heard the lady."

⁓

They never did have that drink. As soon as Abigail opened the door, Time had her pressed against the wall. She wrapped her arms around his neck as his mouth found hers. She leaned into him, molding her softer curves to his hard planes. His mustache and beard whispered against her face's sensitive skin. She enjoyed the contrast of sensation. His lips were cool, firm, and pliant. She could lose herself in his kisses. There was so much he conveyed with his mouth. Lust. Pleasure. Love.

She moaned as his hands caressed the soft weight of her breasts. He was gentle as he pinched and pulled her nipples through the fabric of her dress. Suddenly, her clothes were too tight for her comfort. She wanted ... No ... needed to be skin to skin with this man.

She jerked the tails of his shirt from his pants and slid her hands beneath. His warm skin met her eager fingers.

Time's muscles bunched and flexed at her exploration. She skimmed her nails over the soft hairs on his chest—a nice contrast to his smooth, hard skin.

"I love your touch," he mumbled against her lips.

"Yes," she agreed as she worked at his pants.

He hiked up her dress, nudging her panties aside to flick over her heated core. Her world narrowed to the varied sensations: His mouth on hers, his hand on her breasts, and his fingers inside her.

It had been so long. For a moment, Abigail's panties tightened then snapped as Time ripped them from her body.

"I'd have taken them off," she said with a breathy giggle.

"My way was better." He dropped to his knees, spread her lips, and licked.

"Oh," was all she managed to gasp. When was the last time a man went down on her? And how had she not experienced this before?

"You taste so good."

The vibrations of his voice danced over and through her vagina. She couldn't have replied to save her life. She was swimming toward orgasm. He licked and lapped, sucking her little pearl until she whimpered.

Noisy slurps and breathless moans bounced off the ceiling and echoed back. Abigail couldn't remember a time in her life when she was so turned on for a man. Of course, she knew what it was like to have an orgasm, but this threatened to derail everything she knew.

He plunged two fingers into her slick channel, thrusting in and out as he teased and licked her clit. Her legs trembled the closer she raced toward the precipice. He added a third finger. She was falling, and her breath was heaving.

A low keening cry left her throat as she slid down the door. Time held her close. "We're too old to do this on the floor." He scooped her in his arms and carried her to the sofa. She barely recognized the coolness of the leather before Time was pressing into her.

"You're so tight," he said through clenched teeth.

"You're so big," she countered. Until Time, she thought men came in one size. Now he was filling and stretching her with his hardness.

He stopped. "Am I hurting you?"

She arched her back, trying to draw him deeper. "No. Don't stop!"

"Yes, ma'am." He continued to enter her slowly.

"Time. You're killing me." She shifted, doing her best to impale herself on his hardness.

He gripped her hips. "Be patient. I want to make this good for you."

No matter how she moved, his strong hands kept her still for his slow, easy thrusts. She'd never been so full before. He touched places in her she never thought possible and savored the tiny jolts of electricity racing through her veins and igniting pinpricks of pleasure everywhere Time touched.

Slowly he moved in and out. The velvet encased hardness rasped over every sensitive nerve, and another orgasm began to form. Tension coiled and tightened with every stroke of his hips. Their intimate joining was her sole focus. If the moment left her dead, she would be content.

The soft slaps of flesh on flesh filled the room, and the sofa creaked with movement.

Abigail reached up to trace the contours of Time's face. Sweat beaded his wrinkled brow. She skimmed her fingers over his beard, tracing his full lips tense with concentration. As Time moaned his pleasure, his warm breath hissed against her palm.

Time was enjoying this as much as she was. Somehow, she managed to hook her ankles at the small of his back as he pounded into her. He flexed his pelvis, and her world tilted and slid off its axis. The climax blew through her with the force of a tsunami. Waves of pleasure swamped, drowned, and shoved her back out. Above her, Time roared before collapsing next to her.

Time had never cum that hard before. Every bone and muscle in his body seemed to be made of putty. All he could do was pant and inhale the perfume of good sex. He became aware of gentle fingers combing his hair and caressing his shoulders.

"You were absolutely amazing," he murmured, stroking her breast.

She shuddered beneath him. "I think I died and went to heaven."

"I know I have," he chuckled. He shifted Abigail until she was sprawled atop him. "You beautiful woman. I was trying to do this the right way, but you're so enticing."

She snuggled against him. Strands of her silky hair tangled in his beard. "And what's the right way?"

"Marry me."

At her sharp inhalation, Time held his breath.

"Are you serious?"

"Baby, I'm too old to be playing games." He swept a damp curl from her face. "I want to wake up to you every day and go to sleep with you at my side. I want to make love to you when the fancy strikes and hear you scream my name."

Color rushed into her cheeks.

"No one but you has ever made me feel this way."

"But it's so sudden," she stammered.

"Is it?"

Whether she knew it or not, she had a very expressive face. So many emotions darted over her features: Love, uncertainty, and hope.

"I've only told my daughter we were dating," she began slowly.

"If they want to sit down and talk with me, I'm open to the idea. I don't want to come between you and your children."

Abigail thumped his chest. "You sound so reasonable."

"I'm a reasonable man in love with a feisty woman. I'll do anything to make you happy," he vowed.

Tears glimmered in her brown eyes while a smile curved her delectable mouth. "Of course, I'll marry you."

Chapter Eight

Abigail couldn't stop smiling as she mixed drink after drink. As usual, the Thursday night crowd was three deep at the bar. These were mostly her regulars interspersed with a few new voices. She zipped back and forth behind the waist-high counter. On each pass, a whiff of sweet roses broadened her smile. The floral arrangement stood out of the way on a shelf on the back counter. A second arrangement sat in her office.

Time was too good to her. And each time she smelled the flowers, she thought of him and the fantastic night and morning they had shared.

"Abby, darling!" a cozy Southern-tinged voice called. "You're looking radiant."

"Stx." Abigail finished pouring a beer and set it on a napkin and tray. "You here for open mic night?"

He tapped a staccato beat on the counter. "Yeah. Me and my buddies are gonna take the stage in a bit."

"Cool."

"Hey? Does your group have any upcoming events where you need some sighted volunteers?"

"We've got the wrestling match this weekend. And we have a meeting this weekend. I'll keep your name in mind if there are any scheduled adventures."

"Sounds like a plan," Stx said. "Catch ya later."

Frantic pounding accompanied the ringing of his cell. Time fumbled the phone, pausing to answer. "Fath—"

"Oh my god, Mr. Time. Please open the door."

Time looked from the phone to the door as the panicked female voice came through in stereo. He walked to the door and twisted the lock. Someone shoved the wood open, and a disheveled woman fell into the room. He squinted at the shaking, sobbing woman.

The typically lacquered hair was limp and hanging around her shoulders. The conservative navy dress was wrinkled, the belt missing a loop, and some buttons remained unfastened.

Time poked his head out the door, glancing left and right. Nothing, and no one, was out there. He closed and locked the door.

"Mrs. Johnstone?" he asked cautiously.

Nodding, she tried to stand. After a couple of feeble attempts, Time grabbed her by the elbow and hauled her to her feet. He led her to a chair and offered her the box of tissue. He'd never seen Abelene Johnstone in such a state. She was always prim and proper, as if she stepped off the cover of Old Maid monthly. To see her with streaks of mascara, faded lipstick, and her hair wild was disconcerting.

"I am so sorry for barging in like this." She dabbed at her eyes, which did nothing for the black lines running down her cheeks, then blew her nose.

He swept a hand toward a partially open door. "There's the powder room if you'd like to take a moment to compose yourself. I'll get us some water."

"Thank you," she said quietly and shuffled toward the bathroom.

Time waited until the door closed before he moved to his kitchen. Why she hadn't gone to his office went to her state of mind. He returned to the front hall and placed the glass of water on the side table next to the chair.

He occupied the matching chair as Abelene emerged from the bathroom.

What a difference five minutes made. Abelene had cleaned up, applied fresh makeup, and tamed her wild hair into a simple French twist. Time sniffed the air. If he wasn't mistaken, a bit of eau de cologne perfumed the air. He handed her the water. "Better?"

"Yes. Forgive my intrusion. I was so flustered; I didn't know what to do."

"What happened?"

She took several tiny sips of water before responding. "I think." The hand holding the glass trembled.

Time removed it from her fingers before she could drop it. A tingle raced up his arm. *Fear.* Overwhelming fear assailed him.

"I think someone tried to kill me."

By the time Time coaxed the full story from his client, images were sliding through his mind as if they were on a screen.

"I'm going to contact a friend of mine," he explained. "He's a very nice policeman, and he will make sure you get home."

Abelene clutched his forearm. "What if I'm not safe at home?" Her brown eyes widened in panic.

"Sgt. Falls will make sure you are safe." Time fished his phone from his pocket and tapped on the policeman's name. He quickly relayed his dilemma. A moment later, he concluded his call. "I believe I know who your father is."

The brown eyes widened in wonder. "Really?"

He nodded. "All I ask is you give me another 24 hours to confirm this last detail."

"Of course."

Thirteen minutes later, Sgt. Falls arrived on Time's doorstep. "You always keep things interesting, old man," Falls said with a grin. "You know this is my day off."

"I thought about your partner, Potter, but he strikes me as an incompetent hothead."

"He's on leave at the moment." The answer was tight and strained. He nodded toward the seated woman. "Your client?"

Time nodded. "Yes. Abelene Johnstone."

"I got a look at your vehicle," Falls began. "I'd like you to take me to the spot where it happened."

Abelene clutched her purse. "In my vehicle?"

Falls offered her a gentle smile. "No, we'll take mine. If you don't mind, I'll have a couple of colleagues find what they can from your vehicle." He held out an arm.

Abelene placed her hand in the crook. "Thank you, Sgt. Falls."

Time trailed them to the door. "I'll be in touch."

He closed and locked the door. The visions bombarding his mind when he touched Abelene were enough to solidify his hunch and the research he'd done at the library. Now, he needed to meet the man in question to confirm his findings.

He picked up the phone and dialed his driver. "Could you be out front in five minutes?"

"Of course."

Hanging up the phone, Time picked up the stack of envelopes and the pages he'd printed out. He stuffed the items in his pocket as he picked up his cane. *This is going to be very interesting.*

⌒

"Mr. Time," Thomas McBride greeted. "What brings you to my humble abode?"

Swift followed the elderly man into a pristine parlor. Two high wingback chairs flanked a decorative table. It looked like crystal or glass chess pieces were scattered on the black and beige board. He couldn't quite decipher what color the walls were. They could be anything from white to taupe. Filmy curtains framed the large windows, and sunlight streamed through the panes.

"I believe my client has been searching for you?"

Thomas's lined face creased in puzzlement. "Why would I come up in your investigation?"

Swift pulled the stack of letters from his pocket and handed them to the man.

With shaking hands, Thomas accepted the bundle. Tears misted in his eyes as he looked at the faded words.

"Wh-where did you find these?" He cleared his throat, but it still stuck with emotion.

"My client. She was raised by her mother, whom she, my client, now believes is her aunt."

"Ginny," Thomas supplied. "I was in love with Edna. I was going to marry her when she told me about the baby, but she didn't want to be a war widow." He managed a self-deprecating smile. "As you can see, I survived the war."

"Thank you for your service."

Thomas waved the comment away. "By the time I returned, Edna had the baby and was married to the local butcher. She gave the baby to Ginny to raise."

"Did you have any contact with either of the sisters?"

Thomas shook his head. "She'd moved on, and I lost touch. Because of my injuries, I was in no position to raise a child." He handed the letters back.

"You changed your name."

"My mother remarried, and her husband adopted all five of us. My father ran out on us when I was 13."

Time digested this information. "Does anyone know you were looking for your daughter?"

"Funny you should ask. I told my son Cain to find her. My wife knew I had a child, but we were busy starting our own family and business."

"Why now?" Time wondered.

"I'm not getting any younger. When Edna died, I thought it long past time to find my daughter."

"When I took this assignment, I wasn't even sure I would find you. Now, I can go back to my client and tell her you are real, and you want to meet her."

Thomas blinked, and tears fell from his eyes. "She's alive? And looking for me?"

"Yes."

Thomas placed a hand over his heart and bowed his head. "Do you think she will ever forgive me?"

"Do your other children know of her?" Time deflected.

"I mentioned her in passing, but the only one who knows all the details is Cain."

"Is he your eldest?"

A watery smile broke through. "No. He's my baby boy and the one who will take over the company when I'm no longer able to run it."

Tingles raced and snapped through his synapses as images he couldn't grasp floated like ash on the wind. Time closed his eyes and breathed deep and slow. "I take it your son has worked every department in the company?"

"Absolutely! How can you tell a man or woman their position if you've never worked it? And just to keep those skills sharp, he rotates through departments about once a year." Pride colored his voice. "Just as I've done every year since I started the company."

Time sat back, working on the best way to compose his next question. "Does this mean all of your children have an equal interest in the company?"

Thomas nodded. "Every single one of my children has an equal stake in McBride's Baking Company. When my Edna died, I made sure my will included my long-lost daughter."

"Did you tell your son this?"

"Of course. I have no secrets from my children."

Time stared at him.

"At least not anymore."

Time stood abruptly. "Thank you for your time, Mr. McBride. I will contact my client and give her your information."

Thomas slowly pushed to his feet, using his cane as leverage. "Has someone..." He shook his head. "Please have your client contact me. I'm very eager to meet her."

They walked toward the front door.

"I want—I need to explain what happened and why I wasn't there."

"I understand." Time grasped the knob. "Once I'm back at my office, she will have your information."

Thomas clasped his hand. "Thank you, Mr. Time. Thank you for finding my daughter."

Time grinned. "My pleasure."

Turning, Time bounded down the steps. He didn't wait to get to his office. He called Abelene from the back of the chauffeured vehicle and relayed the information. Time dropped his phone back in his pocket. There was still time to swing by the restaurant and see Abigail.

Music, laughter, and scattered conversation assaulted Time's senses. He wove his way through the crowd to the back office, where the noise sounded like a dull roar. He knocked on the closed office door.

"Come in!"

Time twisted the knob, slipped through the opening, then leaned against the closed door.

And there she was, sitting at the computer, inputting numbers. The mechanical voice spoke so fast that Time could barely catch every other word.

He knew the exact moment she realized it was him. Her long, slim fingers hesitated above the keys, and a slow siren's smile creased her lips.

"Swift." She rose, pushing the chair back. "Thank you for the flowers." She crossed to him and placed her palms on his chest.

"You are more than welcome, my angel." He tilted his head, feathering a lingering caress over her lips.

She made a moan of pleasure that shot straight to his groin. He cinched her closer, feeling her arms tighten at his waist.

He lifted his head, loosening his grip just in case she wanted to step back.

"Did you have a good day?" Abigail asked. "Would you like something to eat? I can grab something from the kitchen for you."

Now that he thought about it, he was starving. At the mention of food, his stomach growled and cramped in protest.

"Got one of them Philly sandwiches on tap?"

"I think we can accommodate you." She turned in his arms and touched a button to the left of the door.

A deep male voice crackled through the intercom. "Whatcha need?"

"Bring two Philly steaks with fries. Extra meat and cheese on one, please."

"Will do. Anything to drink?"

"Coke for both," she stated.

"I'll rush it through," the disembodied voice promised.

She released the button, rubbing her cheek against Time's shirt. "You always smell so good."

"I'm glad you approve."

Abigail lifted on tiptoe to press her mouth to his. "We can eat out on the patio. There's a private section with heaters and such."

"Will your crew know to bring it out there?"

She twined her fingers with his as she opened the door. "Oh, sure."

Abigail led Time down the hall. A fast bass line vibrated through the walls and floor while muted clinks of silverware on glassware accompanied the whoosh and thrash of the commercial dishwasher. Abigail's pride swelled and threatened to overwhelm her.

Once again, she would share her life with a man who meant the world to her. He didn't mind her choice of career. She actually envied him a little. *A wrestler and a private investigator?* That was like the romance trifecta, especially when factoring in love. Oh, and how the man had loved her.

Heat bloomed in her cheeks as she recalled how well he loved her last night and this morning. Everywhere he touched still tingled.

"You're thinking about me," he teased, his breath hot on the back of her neck.

"And how do you know that?" She led him through a set of double doors, crossing an expanse of concrete sprinkled with rough patches. It was just enough space for Abigail and other visually challenged individuals to make their way through the room.

Chilly air wrapped around them, but as they neared a corner table, warmth beckoned.

"Here we are." She patted the table before sliding into a chair. Time sat across from her, still holding her hand.

"Your skin is always so soft." Time raised her hand and kissed her knuckles.

Abigail blushed as her belly did a slow fizz. "I love how you love me."

"You ain't seen nothing yet, love."

Hinges moved, and shoes squeaked across the concrete. "I've got your food," a friendly male voice announced. "Who gets the extra meat and cheese?"

"Time," Abigail answered.

The server slid plates, glasses, and silverware in front of Time and Abigail. "Ketchup and steak sauce are in the middle of the table. Do you need anything else?"

Abigail unrolled her napkin. "No. We're good."

"Bon appétit."

Footsteps faded as Abigail cut the sandwich's toasted bread, melted cheese, and tender meat in quarters. Reaching for the ketchup, she brushed Time's fingers as he grabbed the steak sauce. She poured a liberal amount of ketchup on her plate and set the bottle back in place.

"Is everything okay?"

"Mm-hmm."

Abigail smiled. She could hear him chewing, and she caught him with a mouthful. She bit into her sandwich, savoring the well-seasoned ribeye, mushrooms, peppers, and onions.

"This hits the spot," Time said when his mouth was free. "Sharing a meal with you certainly changes my whole day. I could get used to this."

"Me too."

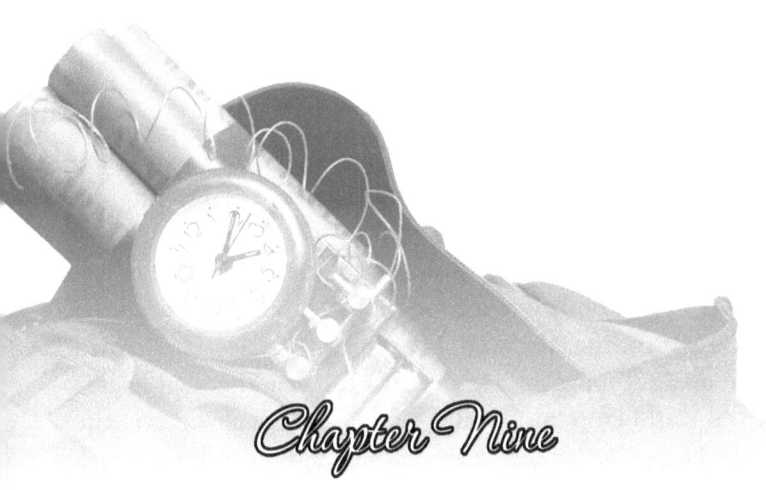

Chapter Nine

Faa-ther Time! Faa-ther Time! The excitement and electricity of the crowd were palpable. Time stood waiting for the right moment to emerge. Time held a tall wooden staff in one hand while the other held the elbow of his guide for the night, Joshua Hastings.

"Nervous?" Joshua asked, his Southern drawl in full effect.

"Not at all." After releasing Joshua, Time straightened the hood on his long cloak. "For fifteen minutes, I get to stop being Swift and become Father Time. Listen to the crowd."

Cries of Father Time and Tick Tock echoed throughout the arena. Time paused. "I forgot to tell Abigail I was taking a hit with a chair tonight. Could you tell her for me? I don't want her to worry."

The other man chuckled. "Of course. But I'm concerned about you taking a hit with a steel chair."

Time smiled. "We're professionals. We can take a hit."

Music swelled but was nearly drowned out by the roar of the crowd. Time squeezed Joshua's elbow. "That's our cue." Time relished the brisk walk to the ring. Fingers reached out to touch Time's robe as he passed. He loved this. The energy. The excitement. The electricity of fans shouting and chanting his name.

"We're at the steps," Joshua told him.

Time stood with one foot on the ground and the other poised on the first step. He spread his arms. The crowd roared its approval. He shed his robe and handed Joshua his staff before mounting the steps and vaulting over the top rope. He landed with a bounce and thud. Time struck a pose, showing off chiseled biceps, then in a move that would've made The Rock proud, made his pecs dance. Almost impossibly, the volume in the room doubled.

Time ran the ropes, pausing at each corner to climb to the second turnbuckle and wave his arms in triumph. At each corner, he struck a pose, flexing his biceps and egging the crowd on. By the time he reached the third corner, a low murmur had risen, and the tension in the room shifted. The hairs on the back of his neck prickled. Running footsteps vibrated through the ring, and Time bit back a smile. He knew what was coming. A metallic clang reached his ears, and the crowd screamed. Whether their cries were in protest or warning, he couldn't be sure.

A blur of color caught his peripheral. A blue. Time frowned. *There shouldn't be blue.* A thud behind him. The warnings from the crowd grew louder. Wind whistled at his back, and he dove forward.

The concrete rushed to greet him. He grabbed the bottom rope, throwing his weight forward and beneath. The metal chair clattered to the ring. Time grabbed his assailant's ankles and pulled.

The man fell backward with a thud and bounce. Time scrambled to his feet as the man slowly got to his. He was close enough to recognize the man. And it wasn't the heel who was supposed to be partnering him in the ring.

"Well, Rodney," Time taunted. "You've come for that spanking, I see."

"I'm gonna take you out, old man," Rodney panted.

Time laughed as Rodney rushed him. He caught Rodney in a headlock and used the man's momentum to drive him into a turnbuckle.

Rodney staggered. Time grabbed him, shoving his back in the corner. Taking a handful of Rodney's shirt, Time ripped it to expose bare flesh. He stepped back, swiveled his hips, and landed an open hand smack on the man's chest.

"You've just been Time Stamped!" Time yelled. "Again?" he asked the crowd.

They roared their approval. Time smacked the man's chest again and again. Each time the crowd chanted and counted. When Time reached ten, Rodney sagged. Time lifted the man over his shoulder, crossed to the metal chair, and opened it. Time sat, bringing Rodney over his knee.

"I promised you a spanking." With the crowd laughing and chanting his name. Time proceeded to spank Rodney.

⌒

"I don't think I've ever been so afraid in my life," Abigail admitted later that evening, settling into Swift's strong arms. "When Joshua told me about the steel chair, I was concerned. But when he said Rodney leaped into the ring, I about died."

Swift nuzzled her neck. "My granddaughter warned me something was going to happen. And I knew something other than what we had planned was going to happen. I just didn't think it would be Rodney."

"And the crowd thought it was all part of the show."

"At least until they watch the news."

Abigail trailed her fingers over his lips, his mustache tickling her digits. "You are such an amazing man."

He kissed her fingers. "You humble me. All I do is crack jokes and throw people around a ring."

She chuckled. "You do so much more than that. You bring peace to families and solve mysteries."

"The important thing is how much I love you and want to spend the rest of our lives together."

"And we will. With Rodney out the way, life will return to normal. We won't have to worry about him coming after anyone else."

Abigail placed a kiss over his heart. "Knowing Rodney is locked up eases my mind so much. I don't have to worry about my employees or you being hurt." She drifted her fingers over the dips and planes of his body. "Why would he do such heinous things?"

"He lost everything, so he had nothing to lose." He nipped her ear lobe, shifting until his body blanketed hers. "Let me show you how much I love you."

⌒

Swift Time sat at his desk. Since he'd wrapped up two major cases in the last week, it was time to write up his notes and put them to bed. Besides, he had a date with his beautiful fiancée. Which reminded him... He needed to take her shopping for a ring. They could do that today after lunch. Abigail agreed to meet him at his office. They could go ring shopping from there. He glanced toward the closet and lingered his gaze on the wood before bringing it back to the monitor. He finished typing when the first creak of wood sounded outside his office door.

Swift saved his work as the doorknob slowly turned. A moment later, a medium-height man with a metallic object protruding from one hand stood framed in the entryway. Swift sat back.

"Have you come to kill me, Cain?" Time asked conversationally.

Cain sneered. "You weren't supposed to find her. You were supposed to back off after being shot at," Cain sputtered.

"That was you throwing ball bearings at me?" he scoffed. "You did a lot of property damage just to scare me away."

"Do you know how hard I worked on my father's company? I slaved for years. I spent summers and holidays learning everything I could, and he tells me he's lowering my portion to give to a long-lost sister. How is that fair?" Cain demanded. "You've ruined my life!"

Time tilted his head to the side. "Your life is only ruined if you pull that trigger. When I spoke to your father the other day, he had nothing but great things to say about you and your family. How would it make him feel if he were to learn you contemplated killing me over money?"

Cain's hand wavered. "Stop talking! You know nothing about my family."

"I know your father prizes his family above everything else. He would be destroyed to know his prodigy is so jealous of a woman he's never met that he tried to run her off the road."

"How?"

"Destruction of property and a hit-and-run can be explained away. Cold-blooded murder cannot."

Faint clicking of nails on the linoleum reached Swift's ears. He had to do something before Abigail walked into this very volatile situation. Time placed his palms on the desk. "I'm going to stand up now. I had a match last night, and I'm a little sore." Slowly, he gained his feet, noting how the gun followed his every move. It seemed like Cain knew how to handle the weapon, but Swift knew something Cain didn't.

"I don't want to hurt anybody. I just didn't want… "

"To share the wealth?"

"My siblings all chose their own paths, and they still get a share of the business. I love the company. It's all I ever dreamed about doing."

"And my client only wanted to know her biological father. She was abused during her childhood, had two failed marriages, and lost her mother. She didn't ask for anything from your father. Only to know him."

"Swift?" Abigail called.

A warning growl preceded a scream of pain. The closet door burst open as Time leaped across the desk. The weapon fell to the carpet with a dull thud.

"Oh. My god! Percy! Off!"

The dog continued to growl while the man screamed in pain.

Sgt. Falls reached Cain. Time kicked the weapon to the other side of the small office. Falls shoved Cain against the wall. The seat of his pants was ripped, and blood marred the edges of the fabric.

"He never does that," Abigail sputtered as Percy barked. "What happened? Is anyone hurt?"

Swift folded her in his arms. "It's okay. Percy was protecting me."

"From what?" Abigail demanded in a shrill voice. She dropped to her knees, her hands roving over Percy's harness and coat. He licked her face. "You crazy dog. Who did you bite?" She removed the cloth from between his teeth.

"It's okay, Abigail," Time repeated.

"Yes, it is. The suspect is subdued," Sgt. Falls stated. "Would you like to press charges, Time?"

Cain was sobbing.

"No. His weapon wasn't even loaded," Time answered wearily. "Just take him and hold him for a little while. Let him think about how bad his life could be behind bars."

"I can do that." Falls led the crying man away. "And we'll get him looked at. Your doggo really took a bite outta crime." Falls left laughing.

"Okay. You're going to have to explain to me what just happened."

"I will. But first, could you remove Percy's harness so I can thank him properly?"

Abigail did as requested.

Time squatted to scratch and pet the dog. "You are such a good boy!" he praised.

"We'll make sure you get an extra carrot for protecting me." Time stood, touching Abigail's arm. "Thank you."

She returned the harness to Percy. "You'll explain everything over lunch?" she prompted.

He wrapped an arm around her waist and pulled her to him. "I love you, Abigail. Let's go find you a ring."

Epilogue

Abigail rubbed a finger across the three-stone diamond ring. The band added a comforting weight to her finger. Voices moved around her as laughter swirled and mingled with the music. They were doing karaoke tonight. The group loved to get up and sing.

"That's a beautiful ring," an unfamiliar female voice said close to her ear.

"Thank you. You must be new here. I'm Abigail."

"Good to meet you, Abigail. I'm August, but everyone calls me Sol."

"Good to meet you, Sol." Abigail smiled. "Oh, Swift invited you to our social night."

"He did," she confirmed. "I had no idea this group existed."

"We have a lot of fun."

"And you own the bar?"

"Yes."

"And you seem happy."

Abigail paused in her response, listening to the tone rather than the words. Was that envy she detected in the other woman's voice? "And you're not."

"Not at the moment. I had to relocate here so I could take care of my son. Actually, it's my ex's son and his wife's son."

"How old?"

"Six."

"What happened that you're raising him?" Abigail ventured.

"My ex and his wife were murdered."

Abigail laid a comforting hand on Sol's arm. "I'm so sorry."

"I'm not. They deserved it," Sol said with such vehemence that Abigail laughed.

"I know that's not funny, but your response was unexpected."

A smile filled Sol's voice. "That's me. Honest and open."

"Don't worry—your secret is safe with me. Next time bring your son. He'd enjoy it, and I love kids."

"Thanks. It's my turn for karaoke."

"Give us a show," Abigail encouraged.

"Who's your friend?" a male voice greeted.

"Oh, Stx, you made it."

"I did, but I'm on call tonight."

"Well, hopefully, you'll get to sing before you leave."

The music changed, and Jill Scott's "Long Walk" rolled from the speakers. A hush fell over the group as Sol's rich soprano filled the room.

"Be still my heart. I think I'm in love," Stx gushed.

Abigail laughed. "She's good."

"Who is she?"

"She goes by Sol, and this is her first social."

"Well, I'm going to introduce myself once she's finished singing."

"Be careful. She has a story to tell," Abigail called after him.

"Are you playing matchmaker?" Swift pressed a kiss to her temple.

"Not at all." She leaned into him. "Did you get it?"

"I did," he confirmed. "As soon as karaoke is done, we will be man and wife." He cinched her closer. "I think that's a very appropriate song."

"I'm ready to take a long walk with you." She laid a hand on his cheek, the hairs of his beard familiar against her palm. She lifted on tiptoes and pressed her lips to his. "For the rest of our lives," she murmured against his lips.

He deepened the kiss, and Abigail knew they'd cherish the rest of their days.

Author's Note

I n this story, Percy, Abigail's guide dog, bites Cain. Guide dogs are not trained to be aggressive or for protection. They are trained to guide their handlers around obstacles and keep them safe in ordinary scenarios. I've met the real Percy, and he's a very vocal character. He loves to talk, and he gets along great with my guide.

So, to reiterate, guide dogs are not trained to protect or defend. But they are dogs and are fiercely loyal to their handlers. Thanks, Mary Ann, for allowing me to immortalize Percy in this series.